THINK FAST, RANGER!

THINK FAST, RANGER!

Will C. Brown

Chivers Press · G.K. Hall & Co.
Bath, England · Thorndike, Maine USA

This Large Print edition is published by Chivers Press, England, and by G.K. Hall & Co., USA.

Published in 1998 in the U.K. by arrangement with Golden West Literary Agency.

Published in 1998 in the U.S. by arrangement with Golden West Literary Agency.

U.K. Hardcover ISBN 0–7540–3191-8 (Chivers Large Print)
U.K. Softcover ISBN 0–7540–3192-6 (Camden Large Print)
U.S. Softcover ISBN 0–7838–8378-1 (Nightingale Series Edition)

The text of this Large Print edition is unabridged.
Other aspects of the book may vary from the original edition.

Set in 16 pt. New Times Roman.

Printed in Great Britain on acid-free paper.

British Library Cataloguing in Publication Data available

Library of Congress Cataloging-in-Publication Data

Brown, Will C., 1905-
    Think fast, ranger! / by Will C. Brown.
        p.   cm.
    ISBN 0-7838-8378-1 (lg. print : sc : alk. paper)
    1. Large type books.   I. Title.
    [PS3552.R739T48   1998]
    813' . 54–dc21   97-44871

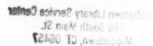

CHAPTER ONE

The prison wagon rolled along like a shrouded wraith in the moonlight, with the road to itself and the Texas countryside sliding past in a peaceful sheen of silver-dappled foliage.

The sandy ruts curled down into a wider town street. The driver slowed the agile mule team and watched the unlighted frame-front stores until these were passed. The guard on the seat beside him held his shotgun half raised and watched both sides, too, with neither of them speaking.

The wagon furnished the only sounds and visible movement within the sleeping village. It rolled the length of the main street, in from the north, out at the south, and into the tree-lined country again.

The driver said, 'Prairieville. That was halfway.'

'Must be two o'clock,' the guard commented. He had relocated the shotgun to his lap. 'We ought to make Huntsville for late dinner.'

'It's the nighttime that's longest.'

'Yeah. This is a delivery I'll be glad to be finished with.'

The driver muttered, 'Me, too,' and touched the whip lightly to each mule to maintain the steady roll behind their trot. The wagon was

1

light and its axles were well greased. Its taut canvas cover had been dyed brown, and the bolts holding the shackle rings along each side of the bed had been painted over in the same color. The rig and mules showed almost earth color in the faint light of the quarter moon, and there was no white anywhere about to advertise them.

In a moment the driver asked, 'How's our boy back there?'

'Sleepin', last time I looked.' The guard twisted about to look again. It was nearly pitch dark under the wagon cover. The guard had to peer hard for several seconds until his vision could make out the form on the blanket pallet in the wagon bed. The figure's right wrist was connected to a shackle ring by a slack length of chain and the leg irons showed dimly at his ankles.

The guard said, 'Still sleepin', looks like.' He added bitterly, 'But he's got a bigger sleep comin', where we're takin' him. The sonofabitch. The goddam murderin' sonofabitch.'

The driver, who considered himself a religious man, said in mild reproof, 'I wouldn't use such rough words on a man, Duncan.'

'Well, that's what he is. I'd like to stay long enough to see the hangin'.'

'Not me,' the driver said quietly. 'It's a terrible moment when a man goes to meet God. Especially for this 'un.'

2

'Well, we all got to do it some day.'

'I know. That's why I wouldn't use blasphemy on one about to do it. Even Prez.'

* * *

The five riders wore no white, either, and were even darker than earth color where they waited in the shadows of the thick-growing live oaks. A running stream behind them made a small, sheltering sound of its own, and the oncoming wagon was barely heard above the spring's busy chattering.

The man who sat his horse a length in front of the four bunched behind him raised his arm in a signal. The others touched the bandana masks tightly shielding the lower halves of their faces. Now they all heard the wagon—the creaking play of leather traces, the mules' trot rhythm in the road just beyond the screen of tree shadows.

The leader abruptly brought his arm sweeping down when the wagon reached a point a few feet short of their hiding place. Knees pressed in upon saddle fenders, hands shook tightened reins, and the raised revolvers glistened when the moonlight caught them as the riders spread and came out upon the road.

The two or three who had the best open shots fired almost in the same instant and the guard was first to go. He half stood from the wagon seat, twisted as if to use the shotgun

3

already slipping from his hands, and then pitched headlong over the right front wheel. His shotgun thudded in the sand beyond his outstretched fingers.

The driver was unbalanced when the mules reared and jerked, and had barely drawn his Colt when the next blast of shots knocked him down to the floor with his head and shoulders hanging over the left wagon side.

One of the masked riders caught the bridle of the near mule and was coaxing the team to stand after its first plunging panic. In a moment the team was quieted, except for a nervous play of their hoofs, and the scene suddenly went still and silent.

A rider dismounted and climbed up on the front wheel hub to look through the cover opening, still holding his sixgun ready. He called back, 'One of you bring the tools.' Then he spoke to the dark interior, 'You all right, Prez?'

The reply came with a moan: 'I'm hurt. One of them bullets hit me in the leg.'

They worked rapidly and efficiently, with two remaining on their horses in the roadway, watching the lane in both directions. The sounds of the chisel, hammer, and hacksaw came dimly from inside.

They lifted the prisoner out over the tailgate and he tried to stand, but sank weakly when his left leg gave way.

'We got to tie up that leg wound,' one said.

4

'He's losing blood.'

One of the mounted men came back from the trees leading a saddled horse.

'Don't know if I can hold on,' the wounded one said. 'Damn it, you bastards ought to have watched where you were shootin'—'

'Shut up!' the leader snapped. 'You'll hang to that saddle till we get you to the first hole-up. Let's make it fast, boys.'

One of them walked around to the left side of the wagon where the driver still hung half over the side. The driver moaned and made convulsive movements with his hands, his fingers crookedly spread like claws. The masked one noticed this, lifted his gun, and sent a bullet into the driver's head from six inches away. He was promptly cursed from the other side of the wagon. 'Damn it, we've made enough racket—you want 'em to hear us clear back to Fort Worth?'

The six rode into the oblivion of the foliage on the west side of the road, and in a moment all sound of their going had faded.

The mule team moved, still unsettled, tugging against one another, finally drifted to the left side of the road, and nervously began cropping at the grass. The driver's bloody head and arms still hung over the sideboards, and the guard lay behind where the faint moonlight softly outlined his corpse in the leafy shadows.

The empty countryside kept its peace, and it was not until well past sunup when an early-riding farmer's boy came upon the prison wagon and the dead men. It was noon when someone finally reached the nearest telegraph by horseback and word was sent both ways, north to Fort Worth and south to Huntsville.

The prison warden telegraphed the Governor in Austin and the Governor sent word for the Adjutant General, commander of the Texas Rangers, to come to his office at once.

CHAPTER TWO

Vic Scott had been warned that the county was Felix Hebron's outlaw empire with a fence of Winchester muzzles around it. The harshness of the land emphasized this on the last dozen miles of his stage-coach trip.

The hardware drummer on the seat beside him muttered, 'Oughtn't to be long now. She's quite a town but hell to get to.'

Vic murmured agreement to that and added to himself, *And hell to get out of, maybe.*

After the Devil River's dry crossing, the country stripped down to thorny brush and mesquite barrens. The barrens were bounded toward the Rio Grande by the gaunt outlines of the Chisos hills. The scene itself was enough, Vic thought, to explain how the Hebron clan could operate out here beyond reach of ordinary Texas law.

6

Finally, beneath one of the rocky ridges bristling with yucca spikes the road snaked into a valley huddle of adobe houses on the outskirts of Angelo. A straggle of shacks in the bleak Mexican section swirled past. The remote brush-country town took form, no easier to the eye than the border country around it.

The driver suddenly yelled and whipped up to a flourishing finale of the tiresome journey from Sweetwater. The lurch of speed almost snapped the passengers' necks but it gave the driver his brief glory moment on main street. The once-a-week run ended in a squeal of hot brakes and a cloud of alkali dust.

The passengers stiffly alighted and spoke suddenly aloof good-bys to one another, strangers again after the enforced physical intimacy of rubbing together three to a seat for eighty-five miles.

Vic Scott covertly surveyed the handful of men who lounged in the shade to watch the coach unload. He dropped back under the guise of adjusting his valise straps, lingering to note the procedures of the other passengers and the looks of anyone who might be on hand to inspect them.

He had almost concluded that none matched the descriptions he carried in his head when delayed movement snagged the tail of his eye.

A slow-moving man of giant frame appeared and filled the station doorway. A sheriff's star

7

was pinned askew to his sweat-circled shirt front. He stepped out, seemingly disinterested in the other arrivals, but examining Vic with a slumbering stare.

Another man, younger and swarthy, appeared like a tardy shadow of the first. His clothes were cleaner, but his shirt front also sported a badge, embossed *Deputy Sheriff.*

Vic's briefing for such an encounter flipped through his memory like turning pages of pictures.

Sheriff Arch Moon. Age about fifty, weight two-thirty, round red countenance matching his name. Distant cousin of Felix Hebron. And Deputy Sam Tabor, background unknown, an import since the county was organized, like as not a fugitive from somewhere. Hebron men, and no help to be expected, nor asked, from either.

Vic offered a short nod. The sheriff blinked. The deputy watched in veiled alertness.

Keeping his tone pleasant enough, Vic inquired, 'Can you gentlemen direct me to the Lehman House?'

The red beef with the sheriff's star put together a slow reply. 'It's the first two-story yonder. You aimin' to stay awhile?'

'Could be.'

'Where'd you come from?'

The big thing now: was it a dumb lawman's curiosity, or had the Hebrons been expecting someone of his description?

8

'Why, I came from Sweetwater since yesterday. Fort Worth, originally.'

That sounded innocent enough. But he saw an unmistakable tightening take hold of the sheriff's big frame.

'What's your business? Drummer or railroad surveyor?'

'No. Cattle buyer.'

'You got the credentials, I reckon, to prove it?'

Vic knew a prod of anger. 'Does a man have to show credentials when he comes to this town?'

'Does if I say so. We don't like certain nosy outsiders come buttin' into our business.'

'Seems to me I just asked directions to the hotel. Is that buttin' in?'

'I don't take no city-dude back talk, neither.'

Vic flipped a sidewise glance which showed him the feel of this encounter had spread. People stopped down the walk and half turned back. The promising sniff of trouble also had reached the street. A few crossing pedestrians changed their courses to see what was taking place with the lawmen and the stranger.

In the moment of this small freeze of attention, doubts clutched his ribs. Was this thick-brained sheriff merely giving him senseless show-off talk, or had he been tabbed before he ever reached the town?

The sheriff said sullenly, 'I'll just take you down to the jail till we get you checked on.'

The proud, lean deputy drifted warily to Vic's left. Tabor's sixgun and holster hung low, tied to his thigh. Moon wore his high-waisted at the overhang of his broad stomach. Then, both the deputy and the sheriff turned to look at a stocky, black-mustached man who approached from an adjacent store doorway.

Vic followed their glances, sensing that the oncoming man had been waiting in the shadows all the time. The stocky one appeared to be in his mid-thirties, hard-muscled, and scowlingly at war with all the world within range of his fast-shifting black eyes. Solid authority was carved in the jut of his chin and the way his teeth fought an unlighted cigar back and forth in an endless duel.

He kept the cigar working as he asked around it, 'What've you got, Arch?'

'This feller.' The sheriff motioned. 'Stranger from Fort Worth, kinda smart-alecky.'

'Answers some description, maybe?'

'I dunno yet. Thing is, Tully, I don't have to take no lip when I'm goin' about my duties as sheriff of this county.'

Vic said, 'No lip intended, Sheriff. I merely—'

'We got to keep a lookout for bad characters, comin' out here on the dodge from somewheres,' the sheriff said petulantly.

The farce of that made Vic want to smile. He took a quick survey of Tully Forester, remembering all he had been told about Felix

10

Hebron's range boss. It was all there, bad blood to the core. He had come a long way to meet this man. But until the right time he would have to pretend ignorance of his identity.

Tully shrewdly sized up the stranger. Finally, his jutting chin jerked a nod. 'Go ahead.'

'All right, mister—down to the jail.'

Vic searched the small circle of faces watching this, and saw no sign of friendliness anywhere.

'This is pretty damned ridiculous, Sheriff. No wonder cattle buyers stay clear of your country.'

The sheriff said, 'Tabor, see if he's got a gun on his hip.'

The deputy reached and lifted Vic's coat tail. 'No gun, Arch.'

'Open his valise.'

Tabor came around. Vic raised his boot and planted it firmly on the top of his valise.

'You'll keep your hands off that.'

Tully Forester grunted, 'Wait a minute.'

The sheriff glanced at Tully blankly and Tully worked a gaze around at the expressions of the men watching. Still speaking around his bobbling cigar, Tully asked, 'What does he say his business is?'

'Cattle buyer, he says.'

Tully worked a different appraisal over Vic.

'I think he looks clean, Arch. Cattle buyers are what we need more of out here.'

Moon said readily, 'Why, I reckon he does.

11

Just wanted to find out. Let him go on his way, Tabor.'

Vic picked up his valise, spoke a clipped 'Thanks!' and walked past the expressionless onlookers.

He crossed the street with the tension still knotting his belly muscles. The familiar new-town, first-day tension and uncertainty. Tully Forester had met that stage with a purpose. And the question he felt following him like a gun in his back, was whether he was watching for anyone in particular, or merely was on hand to look over all the arrivals in general.

In the lobby of the Lehman House, he paused for a quick examination of the shabby interior. The long, timbered room appeared deserted except for two old men in a domino game in the near corner. It could have been any Texas cowtown hotel on a warm afternoon. At the desk he signed the open register: *Victor H. Scott, Fort Worth, Texas.*

The stooped clerk spun the book, read the name, and nodded. He consulted a letter pulled from somewhere and nodded again.

'With the Stone and Chesman Cattle Company, eh? Fort Worth. They wrote for your reservation, Mr. Scott.'

Vic glimpsed the company letterhead. When the A.G. covered a man, he really covered him.

'How far to Felix Hebron's place?'

'Five miles north. His brother would be down at the new courthouse, that's Judge Ed

Hebron, the county judge. But Tully Forester is the man you want to see about cattle. He's Felix's foreman. Think he's in town today.'

'I hope I can be doing some business with them. We're in the market for all the fat beef we can find. Paying top prices. I'm a man easy to deal with.'

He gave Charlie, the clerk, a sly city-slicker wink.

Charlie would have been around long enough to know that here was one of those cattle commission men who would take a small cut under the table and give the seller a loose count, claiming later to his firm that the shortage occurred when the herd was en route. Also, a buyer not too nosy about reworked brands.

The clerk squinted one eye to show that he understood. He then fished around in the key rack. His stepping aside exposed to Vic's view a young woman who worked at a littered office table.

He noted her blue cotton dress, the upper portion of which was adequately filled although her shoulders and neck were slender. He saw the olive tone of her profile, the ugly sleeve protectors and an unflattering eyeshade. She turned to glance up at the new arrival.

The impact of the full view made him falter in reaching down for his valise. Her eyes were dark and observant from wide shadowed hollows. Her expression was reposed, almost

13

indifferent. But despite the eyeshade and her on-guard reserve, she was something unexpectedly refreshing to find blooming in that dusty desert of a colorless office. He wished that her mouth would relax its firmness. She appraised him impersonally, as if she had seen crooked cattle buyers register before. She returned to her smudged ledger pages. His delayed nod of politeness was lost.

The clerk said, 'The porter's out on an errand, Mr. Scott—always is when I need him.'

Then how about Miss Eyeshade showing me to my room?

'That's all right. I can find it.'

He climbed the curving stairway and did not immediately enter the room. He stood back from the window at the street end of the hallway. In a few minutes he saw the hotel clerk emerge to the sidewalk, his hat on and his stride brisk, striking south on the sidewalk. Vic supposed word was on its way to some of the Hebrons. Whether that was good or bad, it was a method of getting the job started.

He let himself into room 24 and locked the door. He tried the knob, testing the lock, and then went over the wallpaper pattern on each side of the large and adequately furnished room, his hands feeling for possible knife-point peepholes. He raised the wall mirror for a glance behind it, and tried the window shades, noting where any shadows of himself would fall at night from the positions of the lamps on the

14

dresser and table. He went into the carpeted hallway and walked quietly along its length to inspect the door at the end and the outside wooden stairway descending to the hotel's fenced rear yard. Returning, he paused to listen where he heard voices of occupants behind a door. Their words did not come through plainly, so the walls and doors were solid enough.

In the room he locked his door again and opened his valise, taking out underwear, a shirt and socks. After changing, he located a pen and ink bottle and, composing carefully, wrote on a Stone & Chesman letterhead:

Paul & Co.
General Delivery
Angelo, Texas

I arrived here today on a buying trip over this region for my firm, Stone & Chesman, and hope to find finished beef for which the market demand is extremely good at the moment. Any co-operation you may be agreeable to giving, leading to fruitful contacts, will be appreciated. I do not know your representative here but was instructed to inform you of my arrival in town. I am registered at the Lehman House, where mail or message will reach me. Angus Gilbert, of our firm, asked me to convey his personal regards.

He read it through critically, then sealed and addressed the envelope. Code-words. Angus Gilbert had warned that Paul & Co.—whoever he was—didn't want the water muddied. So that was that.

He took a few Stone & Chesman printed forms from his bag and scattered them carelessly on the table. He placed the valise under the bed and marked its exact edge and corner positions with penciled dots almost invisible in the rug design.

He eyed the bell button next to the door facing and thought whimsically, if he should ring the bell, which would come up? Charlie, the clerk, likely now returned from his outside business? Or maybe the porter? Or the pretty girl? The clerk or the porter, of course, damn it.

Somehow the strangely appealing looks of her had lingered in his mind, and he thought how that would be displeasing to Miss Ellen Johnston, of the Austin, Texas, Johnstons. There shouldn't be but one pretty girl on his mind and she was Ellen. Her father owned one of the finest homes and the largest law practice in Austin and Ellen wouldn't be caught dead in a book-keeper's sleeve protectors and an eyeshade, or even in last month's dress, he suspected. When he returned from this

16

mission, he probably was going to take the course of least resistance, marry Ellen, and thereby marry the fine home, the whole Johnston family, the ready-made law practice, lifelong security and position. As a son-in-law of Judge Johnston he might have to wear a stout family ring in his nose all his life but he would always be a big auger in the state capital.

So why had he made Ellen so unhappy, even red-faced angry, by taking the out-of-town assignment? She had all but commanded him to resign and move right into her father's law office.

The answer to that eluded him. When he walked downstairs, his glance was drawn to the work table behind the desk for another look at the desert blossom in the eyeshade.

But her eyeshade was removed now. He saw that she was in a low-toned conversation with a thick-shouldered young man with plump features and six-inch sideburns.

The young bull had half draped himself across the counter toward her. Their conversation halted as he approached. The man wore the precisely creased white sombrero of a prairie dandy, a brass-trimmed gunbelt, and a white-butted sixgun.

He turned to the intruder with a belligerent squint. His scowl puffed up the meat around his small angry eyes. He moved three-quarters of an inch to permit Vic to place the key on the desk. Vic smelled the whisky.

The young woman tried a mechanical smile but her mind was still sparring across the fence. The young bull had seemed about to jump it in his fervor.

On a malicious, pointless whim to prolong the Colt-toting Romeo's interruption, Vic asked, 'Could you tell me the direction to the Angelo Saloon, Miss . . .?'

'A block south. This side of the street.'

He liked her slightly husky voice. He guessed the hard-breathing ox beside him liked it, too. He let his glance slide through Romeo as if nothing was there, and said, 'And the post office, Miss . . .?'

'It's a block past the Angelo Saloon, toward the courthouse.'

'Thank you, Miss . . .?' This time he prolonged the dangling question and she had to say, distantly, 'Lindsay . . . Ann Lindsay . . . Anything else, Mr. Scott?'

'The room is quite nice—'

'Thank you.' Her eyes flashed, in resentment or humor—he could not distinguish. She knew he was dragging it out and why.

'Thank *you*, Miss Lindsay. Any suggestions how a strange man in town might spend an interesting evening?'

'There's a public dance at the courthouse tonight,' she said stiffly.

Plump Cheeks tapped Vic sharply on the shoulder. 'Mister, you've gabbed out your time.

18

Now haul freight.'

'Sorry! Didn't realize I was interrupting.' Vic smiled brightly, and said, 'Thanks again, Miss Lindsay. If anyone calls for me, I'll be back shortly.'

Romeo kept his puffed-up scowl working as Vic nodded again and turned for the door. Pausing there, he heard the muttered threat, spoken not too low, 'Ought to cave his teeth in, way he was tryin' to lead up to a date with you.'

Vic heard the girl retort, 'You listen to me, Son Hebron! You don't own everything. I simply won't go to the dance with you if you keep drinking all afternoon and if you don't quit bullying that poor Canary Lenny . . .'

Vic reached the hotel porch, very thoughtful. So Romeo was Son Hebron, the nephew of Ed and Felix. The town-dandy member of the outlaw clan.

As he headed south on the walk, he saw Sheriff Arch Moon and Deputy Sam Tabor approaching the hotel from a distance across the street.

Mentally, Vic called the roll: Sheriff Moon, Deputy Tabor, Tully Forester and the lady's man, Son Hebron. *I'm getting acquainted fast. Four of them in the first hour.*

The thought nagged him that he was somehow disappointed that the hotel girl, Ann Lindsay, was also in the Hebron camp.

Too bad Prez Duvall couldn't be as accommodating as those first four he had met.

19

Prez wouldn't be quite so easy to run across.

Vic Scott felt the hair on the back of his neck tingle unpleasantly. Felt like the whole town was eying him from beneath its slow and sleepy surface. All at once it sunk in—that he was really here, in Angelo. Where the Hebrons owned the law and the Mexicans' vote, and his mission was all but impossible, as he had told the A.G.

All that awaited the bad man, Prez Duvall, back at Huntsville prison was the death scaffold. So what did a crazy killer like Prez have to lose? You couldn't cut through all the Hebron gunslingers to get to him, in the first place. And if you did, how would you get him out? What was another murder or two to Prez, fighting to keep his neck out of the hang noose?

Prez, I wish you would just die on us from the wound you already have.

He moved along, alert to the street, the Mexicans lounging beneath the awnings, the slow movement of horse, buggy and wagon traffic in the long street. Here was a town afraid to talk. The decent ones were afraid to testify in court, for the Hebrons ruled with a vindictive hand. Texas law was a far way east.

Vic found the shack post office, posted his letter to Paul & Co., and looked at his watch.

Four p.m. This was the day and that was the hour. He headed for his appointment at the Angelo Saloon.

CHAPTER THREE

The young Ranger met the old Ranger over a drink at the bar in the Angelo Saloon at five minutes after four and it went off as casually as either could hope for. To any local observers, it was no more than a couple of transients in a chance meeting.

Vic spotted Captain Kincaid in his first sweeping tally of the bar line-up. Kincaid caught him in the bar mirror at almost the same instant.

They barely knew each other. Vic Scott had seen the standoffish veteran only a couple of times at headquarters. The Adjutant General had described the legendary Kincaid to Vic, and had warned that the old-timer did not take graciously to double harness. Kincaid was a lone wolf. The A.G. had cautioned, 'Keep your temper and your diplomacy, Scott. Kincaid resents the idea he can't handle any job alone.'

He managed to stand beside the customer who stood next to Kincaid.

Then it went off naturally. All three got into a casual bar conversation. The local, who turned out to be a lease stockman named Thomas, introduced himself. Then the younger stranger reached across and shook hands with the older stranger, saying his own name clearly for Kincaid's benefit.

Under any other circumstances, Ranger Sergeant Victor Scott would have felt obliged

21

to say something appropriate in deference to Kincaid's rank and reputation, and sincerely meant. You didn't meet a living legend without proper acknowledgment of the privilege.

That would have to be saved for later. Kincaid would be unknown in this region, as he was to the Texas general public. But his name meant something in the tight little inner circle of secrecy that cloaked the Adjutant General's pet Special Service Detail, Texas Rangers. There were hazards enough in the undercover SS work without getting a name advertised.

Vic quickly registered the visible details of the man he had been assigned to work with: gaunt jaws, untrimmed gray mustache, lanky build and firm muscles. Kincaid wore the range clothes of the average transient rider, including a Colt .45 in a worn black holster.

At the same time, Kincaid's rather harsh squint from beneath tangled gray brows was taking in Vic Scott. He would want to know what he had to work with here. He would tally the good but slightly frayed suit, Vic knew, the black pants stuffed in cowman's boots, height not quite up to Kincaid's six-three but muscles and hard poundage tighter packed. Thin brown sideburns, a small scar or two from past troubles, blue eyes deep set and without much expression showing at the moment. Very slight left under-arm fullness, which was his small revolver in a thin canvas shoulder holster; invisible, he thought, but maybe Kincaid caught it.

Kincaid and Thomas were having whisky. Vic pulled on a beer and listened for the drift.

It seemed that Kincaid was in the country to lease a sheep graze and was now proposing that the local man steer him about for a land look. Vic took that as Kincaid's approach to making the first cast for sign on the whereabouts of Prez Duvall.

Thinking to get something established, Vic mentioned, 'I'm buying for Stone and Chesman in Fort Worth. Stocker cows and prime slaughter steers. Maybe we could ride out together ...'

Speaking vaguely across Thomas, Captain Kincaid muttered, 'Well, I don't know,' and went back to his palaver with Thomas. When next the gruff captain spoke to him it was to remark, 'Gets damn warm around here, don't it?' This left Vic wondering if he had said the wrong thing, and if so, what. Even with the necessity to play it cautious, he felt a small resentment. The old man had no need to think that here was an amateur, not dry behind the ears.

He pulled on his brew, looked over the line-up of customers at counter and tables, concluding that on the whole they were a hard-looking lot. Some of them booted, gun-heavy range types, some who looked as if they belonged to the railroad construction camp, a few in town suits and a few Mexicans who

23

drank in the rear apart from the Anglos.

After a minute Kincaid cocked a squint at the younger man and asked, 'Where you staying, Mr Scott?'

'Just checked in at the Lehman House.'

'Well, I got me a room upstairs over the wagon yard office,' Kincaid said. 'Always find me a wagon yard room when I can. It's cheaper. Cheaper and private. Think I'll drift back there and take me a nap before supper.' Since it didn't make any difference to anyone what Kincaid aimed to do, the captain must be telling him to come there after this broke up.

Small things, Vic realized. But you lived by remembering the small things.

The man, Drew Cooper, had missed a small thing, somewhere.

Better to trust nobody. Wrong word at the wrong time could end a man's usefulness, if not his breathing.

Vic finished the lukewarm beer and spoke an indifferent *adios* to the other two. Kincaid was pouring himself another straight whisky, Vic noticed. He made his way through the patrons toward the street door.

The batwings exploded inward. He had to sidestep quickly to get out of the path of the bull-like rush of Son Hebron.

Close behind Hebron came another young man with a coyote face and a fool's grin. Son Hebron brushed blindly against Vic, throwing him off balance. Son showed hard concentration for someone at the front curve of the bar. Recovering his footing, Vic was jostled off balance again by Coyote Face who hurried behind Hebron.

Son was snarling, 'Found you, Canary Lenny, you—'

Vic turned, resenting the elbowing, and saw a slightly built man at the counter spin about with fear draining his fuzzy face.

'I don't want no trouble with you, Son—'

'You want to fight me here, Canary, or outside?'

'You got no right—'

The youth's protest was cut off as Son clawed into his shirt front. A frightened whine died as Son jerked Canary into hitting distance and smashed a heavy fist into his mouth. Canary, released, fell to the floor.

Son puffed his cheeks and looked challengingly about at the unmoving spectators. The fallen man attempted to sit. Son's coyote-face follower brutally kicked Canary in the chest.

Son said, 'Now, Canary Lenny, I *told* you I was gonna whup your ass ever' time I caught you in town—'

Canary tried to scramble back on all-fours. 'You don't own the town—'

Coyote, as if bidding for his leader's approval, raised his boot to aim another kick at the downed youth. Vic, watching, thought grimly that there was none here who would move to stop this. Now nearest among the silent customers, he extended a long reach and pulled Coyote off balance.

'No use to butcher him with your boot.'

Coyote angrily slung his arm, trying to dislodge Vic's grip.

Son Hebron bellied close. His stare narrowed in recognition. 'Oh, the smart guy at the hotel, huh? Mr Fort Worth! You itchin' to buy in on some of Canary's trouble?'

Vic snapped, 'No!' but he saw that the big Hebron nephew wanted to cold-cock him on general principles and was going to take a swing. The roundhouse blow was delivered with drunken ineptness. Vic ducked under it and backed away from Son's following rush. Son bulled in, drew back his right fist, and Vic snapped Son's head back with a short, stiff left under his broad chin.

Then a wildcat-fast charge struck Vic from the rear. Coyote Face had made a running leap, with his knees high planted and his wrists locking about Vic's face. Coyote rode him down in a sprawling tangle.

Vic flung Coyote aside, hitting him twice with fast right jabs as Coyote was dislodged. A small, steel-hard jolt smashed into Vic's spine.

Son Hebron, crazy-eyed and snarling, jabbed him again with his heavy Colt as Vic stood up, trying to turn.

'You just march ahead of me out to the back alley.'

26

Vic was conscious of Kincaid watching from the far end of the bar. And without approval. Even more worrisome to him than Son's sixgun was the warning shrilling in his brain that he should never have got involved in this sorry mess.

'*Son!*' The one word came sharply from the entrance. Both the heavy-breathing Son and Coyote with his bloody mouth, turned instantly, and Vic looked, too.

Tully Forester stood spread-legged just inside the batwings. He still chewed a dead cigar and his eyes whipped. He made one short jerk of his head. Son's shoulders sagged.

'But, Tully—'

'Get for home, Son!'

Son dutifully plodded to the door and out, not looking back. Coyote trailed after him, edging cautiously around Tully.

Vic went to the counter and the barman handed him a wet rag which he dabbed at the small bleeding of his nose.

He saw Tully look over the scene. Then the Hebron foreman motioned to a pair slouched at a table. They arose, adjusted their gunbelts, and followed him out.

Vic saw that everyone in the place was taking him in, some grinning. A man drawled, 'When old Tully speaks, they mind, don't they?'

Vic finished with the bloody cloth and avoided glancing at Kincaid.

The patrons went back to their business,

none offering to speak to him. He said, 'Much obliged,' to the bartender, walked through the open space, and out to the sidewalk.

Footsteps hurried on the plank walk behind him. Vic looked over his shoulder. The man Son had knocked down tried to pass.

'Hold it!' Vic caught his arm.

'Lemme alone!' Canary muttered.

'What's your trouble with Son Hebron?'

'Ain't no worse than *yours* is with him, now. You're a fool to tangle with that bunch.'

'What's he bullyin' you about?'

'Maybe he thinks I seen something,' Canary said guardedly. 'Something them Hebrons wouldn't a wanted me to see.'

'And what might that have been?'

Canary edged away. Fear drained all the starch out of him. 'They want to run me out of the country. I ain't talkin' to you or *nobody*!'

Vic watched him hurry on. Then he saw with chagrin that Deputy Sam Tabor stood across the street and had watched his brief talk with Canary Lenny.

At the hotel desk, Vic asked the clerk without preamble, 'Did Sheriff Moon and Deputy Tabor inquire about me?'

His abruptness caught Charlie off guard. The clerk stuttered over his denial. Vic said shortly, 'Never mind. It's their job to check up on strangers, I guess.'

In a struggle to say something, Charlie told him, 'You ought to take in the big dance, Mr

28

Scott.'

'Might do it. Where?'

'At the courthouse. They moved the benches out of the courtroom. Big time, if you like fiddle music and maybe a little roughhouse on the side. Always a little fight or two to liven things up.'

'Well, I might look in. Time gets dull on a man's hands, traveling around like I do. Guess you couldn't help me turn up a date—some nice girl . . .?'

He tried to see past the clerk, hoping that Son Hebron's girl might spare a glance. She held her attention stiffly on her work but he saw enough to know that her ears were straining with female curiosity.

If anyone should know the Hebrons, or rumors about Prez Duvall coming back, why not the girl courted by the Hebrons' flashy nephew? The idea, born of impulse, seemed worth a play. He became the slick traveling man, the bold one with nothing to lose but an evening.

'What about Miss Lindsay, there? Wonder if she has a date tonight? Would you do an unattached guest the great honor, Miss?'

Charlie turned and cackled. 'You turned down Son, didn't you, Ann? Couldn't hardly afford to show up with no Fort Worth cow buyer, then. Ought to do it anyway—you need to make Son a little jealous.'

Ann Lindsay looked calculatingly at Vic.

29

Something decided itself in a female mind. So unexpectedly that it jolted him, he heard her say flatly, 'Why, yes—I believe I would like to go with you, Mr. Scott.'

No timidity, no show of false modesty over such a casual asking by him and easy acceptance by her. Somehow he knew that dignity and independence were inherent here, that she knew that no man would ever mistake her for an easy pickup.

And immediately, a tingle of warning sounded in his brain.

But he had to say cheerfully, 'Thank you, Miss Lindsay. It will be a pleasure. Shall I call, say, around—?'

'Eight-thirty is all right. I live at Amanda Forester's. That's Mrs. Tully Forester, only they are divorced. Anyone can direct you to Amanda's rooming house.'

'I'll find it. See you then.'

Vic climbed the stairs to his room. Had she accepted too quickly? Did she, like most of the rest of them, work on the side of the Hebron clan?

He entered the room, made a quick examination, found nothing had been touched. So Moon and Tabor had contented themselves with checking on his identity with the hotel clerk.

He returned to the lobby. Ann Lindsay glanced his way. He touched his hat brim to her and received a fleeting smile. She busied

30

herself again in her work almost before he could return the smile.

He stalked to the sidewalk and headed for Captain Kincaid's *cheap* and *private* room over the wagon yard.

CHAPTER FOUR

Kincaid brought over two tumblers and made a small ceremony of the pouring, then replaced the bottle on the bare pine-top dresser.

'What'd they call you? Vic? Man gets lonesome, Vic. All these years I've been a loner. Undercover is a polecat's life.'

'I'm sure your accomplishments are appreciated by the department, Captain.' Vic added pointedly, 'Shall we go over the case?'

'You want glory, you better take a field command. Not in Special Service. In this work, nobody ever hears of you. Way you keep alive. Know what the A.G. had the nerve to say to me? He wanted to know if I didn't think it was about time to have some help on my assignments. I said, green help can get a man killed.'

An old war horse's contempt for a colt lay there between them in the heavy fumes of the captain's smelly brand of whisky, and Vic steeled himself to absorb the needling with a thick skin. This was only a ritual, he told himself. He had to overlook an old man's peculiarities. Kincaid had earned some right to this, through decades of bad men outwitted and his life frequently at stake.

In a moment he said evenly, 'Shall we get down to the case now, Captain?'

Kincaid stalked back to the dresser. This time he did not ask Vic to join him. He came back, loosened his collar, sat on the edge of the bed and rolled a wheatstraw smoke. His fingers were steady. After he licked the paper and lighted, he hooked Vic with his harsh scrutiny.

'Like to know who I'm teamin' with. As I remember, you're a kind of a bookkeeper in the A.G.'s Austin headquarters. Records and that kind of paper business, studyin' law on the side?'

Vic felt his face burn. 'Not exactly. I rode two years on the Mexican border with Captain Dewey and Company B, before transferring to Special Service.'

The critical scrutiny eased a trifle. 'I know Company B had plenty of action.'

'I moved into headquarters two years ago. Being in Austin gave me a chance to start reading law, which is what I wanted.' Vic shifted his legs, feeling the discomfort of a man who disliked to talk about himself. 'The A.G. sent me on a few Special Service jobs.' He added shortly, 'The last was the Big Thickets trouble in East Texas.'

Kincaid stood, digesting that, and looked out the window.

'Now, Scott, I like to know if me and the other man have been briefed on the same things. The A.G. gave you the case in Austin, then he caught me in Waco, so we'd better compare notes. First, who's interested in you here, up to now?'

'Sheriff Arch Moon and Deputy Sam Tabor saw me arrive. Wanted to know who I was and why I was here. Tully Forester was on hand, also. The whole outfit's on edge, naturally.'

'You covered all right in Fort Worth?'

'Stone and Chesman will confirm that I'm their buyer. The A.G. fixed that up.'

'Felix Hebron's sly. We don't ever want to forget that one bloody minute.'

'Do you want me to state the case, Captain, as I have it?'

'Go ahead. I'll cut in if I have something different.'

'Felix Hebron's bunch runs the county. His family started years ago as hand-to-mouth rustlers, and got a stranglehold long before the county was organized. His top hand is Tully Forester. Felix's brother, Ed Hebron, got elected county judge when the county was formed. Arch Moon is their distant kin. I guess the new deputy, Sam Tabor, is about the same stripe as the rest. There's never been any law out here. Nobody's been up to buckin' the Hebron bunch. Not even a way to bring these outlaws to trial. Witnesses won't come outside for a change of venue.'

33

Kincaid turned and nodded. 'Let's get down to Prez Duvall.'

Vic said, 'Well, I understand that started when Felix Hebron found a bunch of cattle across in Mexico, branded 7 Bar. He and Tully Forester were pretending to buy them from the Mexican owner. When delivery was made at the river, Hebron's bunch just pulled their Winchesters and murdered the three Mexican herders. They got the herd to their range and started reworking the brand to Hebron's Double H. About as bold and bloody a stunt as was ever pulled. I imagine Prez Duvall was one of his top gunmen in that. Prez is the kind that just naturally loves to kill.'

Kincaid ground out his cigarette on the bare plank floor. 'The Mexicans screamed to high heaven, clear up to the U.S. Department of State. You up to date on the fellow, Drew Cooper?'

'I think so. The federals sent an undercover man in here more than a year ago to look things over. Drew Cooper. He was known to me. We rode together once, both of us in Company B. Cooper saved my life in a close fight with some border outlaws. I owe him something for that.'

Kincaid squinted and muttered, 'All right. Go ahead.'

'Cooper left the Rangers and became an undercover U.S. marshal. I never heard directly from him after that. Understand he got

34

married, left his bride at home to take the assignment here to investigate that Mexican cattle steal. He never got out. Somehow, the Hebron crowd caught on to Drew Cooper. When word drifted out of here about a year ago that his body had been found, he'd been dead for days.'

Kincaid moodily gazed out the window. 'Yonder's their fancy courthouse. Beyond it, Judge Ed Hebron's house with a windmill and tall poplars. Travesty on the law.' He stomped to the dresser, poured another drink, and carried it back to the bed. 'Well,' he said, 'go ahead.'

Vic forced patience to show outside, but inside him he was being assaulted by a thousand doubts bordering on alarm.

'Prez Duvall made the mistake of going to Fort Worth. He got spotted and those two Fort Worth deputies tried to arrest him—there'd been a reward poster out for him for months. He killed one of them, but they caught him and tried him and he got the death penalty. For the deputy's murder, that is, not for the Drew Cooper business. Then, a week ago, two guards were taking him to Huntsville prison where Prez had a date with the scaffold. The Hebron bunch jumped them out of Prairieville. Maybe some Hebron money had bribed somebody in Fort Worth for the tip-off on when they were going to transport Prez. Anyhow, they killed the two guards and got Prez out of there. Prez was wounded, because the signs showed later that he had been losing blood when he came out of that wagon.'

Kincaid nodded. 'The Hebron bunch would have to lug him somewhere. So why not all the way back here? Back among home folks. What we figure we got here, Vic, is a bad wounded man, holed up somewhere. If it's a bad wound, which I hope to hell it is, means he's needin' a doctor's attention pretty regular. So we play it he's in or near this rat-nest of a town. Shot bad enough to stay in one place awhile. Question is, where's the place?'

There was a small morose silence. Vic was thinking, *This case is already shot to hell.* They might have whipped the Hebron problem, by some miracle. But they couldn't whip the Hebrons *s* a whisky bottle.

Kincaid asked then, 'What's your specific orders from headquarters?'

'We are to dig in the best we can. Main objective—find Prez Duvall. Get him out. Alive, for the hanging. Or the other way if forced. As a means to get my foot in the door, I'm to be open to a shady cattle deal with the Hebrons. Somehow one of us has got to get on their range for a look—and they don't relish strangers prowling around.'

Kincaid chuckled as if suddenly thinking of something else that amused him. When Vic stared blankly, Kincaid asked, 'What did they tell you about Amanda Forester?'

36

'She's Tully's divorced wife. Pretty, used to be a cabaret singer. Now runs a boarding house. Possible source of information.'

'I understand Drew Cooper thought so.' Kincaid chuckled again. 'You reckon he overdid it with Amanda? Got Tully mad at him?'

Vic said stiffly, 'I had respect for Drew Cooper. If he was making the play to Amanda, I say it was just a part of his work, trying for information. After all, Cooper had a new bride back home somewhere—'

'Tully might still be jealous. He's a mean sonofabitch, whether it has to do with women, cattle or guns. Well, you could try *your* luck with Amanda.'

'Me?' Vic shook his head, frowning.

'Sure. If she's mad enough at Tully and if she liked this fellow Cooper, she could want to get even.'

Tautly, Vic said, 'Not the way I like to go at a case. I've got a girl—'

He hadn't intended to bring in his personal life. But apparently Kincaid had been briefed on that, too. He quickly took it up.

'It's you and Judge Johnston's daughter, back in Austin, ain't it? Big-time folks.' He cocked a significant squint. 'You'll marry a pile of money, and if it's a law practice you want you'd be marryin' into that, too.' Then Kincaid added bleakly, 'Boy, you gonna be fixed for life.'

Abruptly, Kincaid's voice changed from bleakness to harshness. 'With all that waitin' for him back there, I don't imagine a young man would want to take too many risks when the chips was down. Especially with somebody like the Hebrons—'

Vic found himself on his feet. He stifled an angry rejoinder, trying to remember that there was no use to argue that subject with Kincaid.

He moved to the window and behind him Kincaid asked sharply, 'What about other contacts? You briefed on Paul and Co.?'

'They're our only contact at the moment. It's only one man, really. Paul and Co. is the cover name for a U.S. deputy marshal who's here somewhere. I was told to use the contact sparingly, and only in an emergency. Paul and Co. is playing his own game, a risky one for him, and his department doesn't want elbow-rubbing with the Rangers unless we're in bad trouble.'

'The A.G. may know who he is,' Kincaid said, 'but the federals wouldn't let him tell us.'

'Apparently the Paul and Co. fellow is working on the Mexican cattle steal and Drew Cooper's death, the federal angle on that—not on Prez Duvall, like we are. The federals are pretty scratchy about keeping their man protected.'

Kincaid said, 'Don't blame them, after what happened to Drew Cooper.'

'I was just to notify Paul and Co. that I was

38

here, with the pickup to be general delivery, Angelo post office. The code identification is "Angus Gilbert." The federal is not to reply unless he has a special reason to. That's all I know about Paul and Co.'

'Matches with what I was told, and I was to do the same thing, and have. So the Uncle Sam boy knows we're here. We won't muddy his stream unless they get our backs to the wall. What else?'

'The doctor angle. Especially a veterinarian, Dr. Flayhorn. Does work for the Hebrons. Prez Duvall took a bullet in that escape. Some sawbones should be looking after him.'

'Well, you work on that, Vic.' Wonderingly, Vic saw that Kincaid's hands were still steady enough. Except for a deeper huskiness, his voice worked all right, too. The famed undercover Ranger must be as tough in his gullet and stomach as he was in his gun hand. 'Also, try Amanda Forester, and the cow-buyin' act with Felix Hebron. I'll be nosin' around the country in my own way. I got my way of doin' a thing. When we meet, do it accidental and be damn careful.'

Kincaid motioned to the window. 'When I'm in this room, or needin' a contact with you, there'll be a pair of socks hangin' up to dry in the window . . . Now, how about a little snort before supper?'

Vic edged to the door. 'I'd better get along now, Captain.'

Kincaid stood and frowned. 'Hell, don't get the idea I hit this stuff *regular!* I'm just sort of killin' time today, here on the beginnin' of a case—'

'No, sir,' said Vic with a tight, polite smile. He wanted out of there, and hastily thought to say, 'It's only that I'm taking a girl to the dance tonight. She works at the hotel—Ann Lindsay.'

Kincaid fingered his chin. 'Ain't that the name of Son Hebron's girl?'

'Oh, you've heard that? Well, I thought if she stood in with the Hebrons, maybe she might furnish our first clue by accident, some gossip about Prez—'

Kincaid did not look pleased. 'Son Hebron was the one you raised your hackles over at the saloon. I reckon you know that. Tully Forester broke it up, which was lucky for you. I just hope to God you didn't tip our hands!'

'Why, how could that—?'

'Reckon not. But it put a lot of attention on you.'

'You saw how it came about, Captain. Nothing in that to tip our hands.'

Kincaid trudged toward the dresser. 'A green hand can make mistakes.'

Vic whirled in anger. 'At least, Captain, I was sober!'

Kincaid took his drink in silence, his back turned. Vic eyed the door, regretting his flare of anger. Kincaid came back and took his two gunbelts from the bedpost with affectionate old

40

hands, fumblingly toying with the butts of the holstered .45 Colts.

'Know the best partner a man can have in this business, Vic?' He belched and patted the guns. 'These here little fellers right here.'

CHAPTER FIVE

With the prairie dusk came the first scattered gleams of coal oil wicks newly lighted over the town, and the street scene from the hotel porch stirred itself out of the warm lethargy of the day.

Watching the scene, Vic Scott noticed that the windows were ablaze with lights in the courthouse at the far end of the street. He remembered the border axiom that days were for dozing, nights for fandangoing.

The hardware drummer, settling in a rocker beside Vic, remarked, 'Could be a night for this town to howl. Back you out looking in on the dance, maybe picking us up a couple of calico chicks.'

'Already ahead of you. Got a date with the girl who works here at the hotel.'

The drummer whistled low. 'Man, you work fast. I've heard she's Son Hebron's girl. Funny thing, too, because she looks smarter than that.'

'Well, evidently Son didn't have his acreage posted.'

'If I was you I'd hope Son took his jiltin' in good humor. I heard around that you had a little set-to with him in the saloon.'

'It wasn't much.' Vic decided to take a chance. The Prez Duvall escape was the big news topic back east, anyhow. 'What've you heard about Prez Duvall—wasn't he from around here?'

'Nothing!' the drummer replied emphatically. 'Nobody wants to talk about it and I sure don't try to force the discussion. I try to mind my own business when I'm in Angelo, and damned glad when I get out of here. You never know when you're talking with some Hebron connection.'

As the drummer idly talked, Vic noticed a lamp glow behind a window shade on the distant wagon yard's second floor. Captain Kincaid rejoining the living; with a mouth taste like a crowded corral, likely. But he pulled his thoughts away from that like backing up from yucca spikes.

The yellow gleams in the dusk looked neither hospitable nor like gay beacons to a pleasant night. Somewhere, a lamp should be sputtering over Prez Duvall, bedded in some secret hole-up with his bullet-torn flesh. Perhaps with some shadowy set of hands this minute changing bandages for the night.

Whose lamp? Whose hands? The Hebrons' doctor? Some woman kin? Or hired-man amateur?

42

The A.G. had said, 'You and Kincaid are apt to *feel* the clue that counts, rather than see it. You know what I mean. What you smell in your pores. That's the knack that counts when the law can't go around openly asking questions. Could be one little sniff of a hunch would lead you to Prez.' He had added thoughtfully, 'Even then, of course, your troubles will be just beginning.'

Vic had felt nothing in his pores as yet; no sniff of a hunch. The only reaction to now, he thought, was that of facing the impenetrable wall which was all Angelo and the Hebron iron-fisted rule.

He saw that the first buggies and saddle horses were arriving and being hitched on the courthouse grounds. A straggle of railroad construction workers, who were Southwest Texas's grudgingly tolerated aliens at the moment, came in afoot toward the saloons and stores from their tent camp to the west.

Sheriff Arch Moon sat on the edge of the walk in front of the bank, whittling and talking to a pair of squatting cowhands.

Six riders floated in from the dusk at the north end, taking the middle of the street. They rode in loose formation, two jaggedly abreast, shoulders slackly swaying, all hat shadows and dark features. Tensing, Vic made out the Double H brand on the horses.

He kept his eyes on the stocky man riding front left. Black hat cocked, dead cigar working

43

under a trimmed mustache. Vic held his gaze on Tully Forester until the six riders had jangled past the hotel porch. Tully raised a careless hand to Sheriff Moon, and Moon waggled his knife in a return salute. The men dismounted and tied two blocks down the street in front of the Cactus Queen.

The drummer commented, 'That was a hard-looking bunch if I ever saw one. You notice those riders?'

'I noticed.'

*   *   *

Tully Forester, with his black hat pushed back, stood at the far end of the bar in the Cactus Queen.

Vic made his way toward him. The Hebron foreman faced front, talking idly with the barman. As Vic neared, Forester's sharp eyes narrowed, then turned belligerently questioning as Vic halted. The other Hebron riders held covert attention on him without noticeably changing their mumble of bar talk.

'Mr. Forester?'

The foreman held his unblinking hostile stare as he nodded.

'I'm Victor Scott. Buyer for Stone and Chesman, Fort Worth.'

Forester took his time responding to Vic's proffered hand. One of his riders began to edge that way. Vic saw Forester's cold sidewise

44

dismissal of the man who moved back to his place at the bar.

Forester said shortly, 'Think we ran into one another earlier today.'

'Yeah. When I came in on the stage, and in that little ruckus at the Angelo Saloon. Didn't know who you were, then. Sorry about the run-in with Son Hebron.'

Forester looked him over again. 'Stone and Chesman. Kinda high and mighty outfit, ain't they? Don't think they've had a buyer come out this far before.'

'Well, we're after all the beef we can find and I'd like to get a shipping herd together. Intended to ride out to your place tomorrow and see what you've got to offer.'

'Heard you took pains to let the Hebrons know you'd hit town.'

Vic strained to find any hidden significance in those words, but could not be sure. Anything Forester said was bristling with suspicion and unfriendliness. Toughness, force and vengeance were brand marks showing all over Tully.

'We've got a little stuff we might turn loose, if the price is right. Felix don't much like to haggle with troublesome buyers.'

'I've got a free hand. It's the only way I work. I carry a fresh checkbook, and I'm a buyer who can get along with the seller.'

Forester gave him a new appraisal. 'You make it sound interesting. How come you're so itching for Hebron beef? Buyers've been circlin' around us like we had a polecat smell.'

'Beef's just beef, to me. I'm a man that likes to make a trade. I've heard plenty about the Hebrons, but never that old Felix was anybody's fool.'

Forester at last withdrew his bristling scrutiny. Vic could not tell if the man was satisfied.

'You know where our place is?'

'Five miles north, they've told me.'

'No, that's headquarters. No use to go there.' Forester worked his cigar and Vic studied him narrowly, wondering, *Why not go there?*

'The stuff I'll show you is grazin' in Bitter Creek flats. You bypass the headquarters, ride direct to the graze.' He added details of directions.

It sounded like an evasion and Vic decided that he should push it, but not too far. 'I'd hoped to call on Felix Hebron—we have a mutual friend or two in Fort Worth—'

'Who?'

Vic was prepared with the names of buyers for a shady commission house. Forester made no comment at once, but finally said, 'Well, if Felix wants to see you he'll say so. Can you make it by the middle of the afternoon tomorrow? We'll be pushin' the stock to water.'

Vic agreed and Forester made a head motion toward a table. A man watching from there got up and came over. He was a

Comanche-featured young rider with popped black eyes. Like the rest of the Hebron group, he was armed with a holstered sixgun.

'Chock, this feller is Victor Scott, cattle buyer from Fort Worth. He's coming out to look at some stock. When you sight him riding along Bitter Creek, show him the way in.'

Chock memorized Vic with his peculiar gaze and nodded. 'I'll know him, Tully.'

With that attended to, Forester appeared finished with the conversation and Vic sensed that the meeting had come to a dead standstill.

He offered, 'Join me in a drink, Forester?'

'Don't use it.'

Vic chuckled. 'No bad habits, eh?'

'Oh, I might have a few.' The stocky man made a grimace. 'Had a wife once, she thought I had a hundred.'

Vic felt a stir among the patrons and shot a glance toward the entrance. Son Hebron came swinging in with his bull-heavy plod. Vic took his elbow off the bar and set his leg muscles. Son drew up and gave Vic an angry glare of recognition. Forester grunted, 'Hello, Son.'

Peevishly, the big youth asked, 'When you going back to the ranch, Tully? Tonight?'

'Yeah. You better get on out there. Your Uncle Felix is wantin' you.'

Son said crossly, 'I'm staying with Uncle Ed tonight. Always some damn trouble or other, with Felix out yonder or Ed here in town.'

Sharply, Tully asked, 'Any *new* trouble?'

47

Vic, caught between them but being ignored, thought, *Keep talking, you fat fool.*

With another sour look at Vic, Son muttered, 'Talk to you in private, Tully . . . This is the Fort Worth buttinsky, ain't he?'

'His name's Scott. Cattle buyer from Fort Worth.'

Vic extended his hand. Son ignored it. Tully worked his cigar, watching them both. Vic felt all the other veiled eyes on him, too.

Son said, 'Mister, I just advise you not to show up at the dance tonight with Ann Lindsay.'

A snakes' nest of jealousy already was stirred up in Son, and was apparent to Vic. He had made a mistake in dating Ann Lindsay, but at the time the prospect for information had seemed worth the try. Now it was too late to back out. He tried to keep his voice easy, saying, 'Afraid it's a little too late for that, Hebron. I'm due to call for her in half an hour.'

Tully growled, 'Come over here, Son.' He led the way toward the back corner table and Son followed like a led steer. They gave no further attention to Vic. He walked out, passing through the suddenly silent patrons, and paused on the walk to take a deep gulp of the fresh evening air. What was the trouble that was keeping Son in town, spending the night with his Uncle Ed? And what manner of violence had he invited from Son by impulsively dating Ann Lindsay for the dance?

48

Then it struck him more forcibly than ever that the office flower in the hotel had been entirely too easy, had given him the date too readily.

CHAPTER SIX

Amanda Forester followed them to the veranda of her boarding house after Ann Lindsay had made brief introductions. Vic was surprised to find that the ex-wife of Tully Forester was no older than himself, and that traces remained of her youthful beauty and show-girl grace. She was saying, 'I'll be there after awhile and I'll expect to have a dance with you, Mr. Scott. A new man in town is fair game, you know. Ann, you won't mind?'

Amanda had an engaging smile and knew how to use it. Vic let his glance linger until he was sure his own interest registered. Ann Lindsay said thinly that she wouldn't mind.

Vic escorted her to the hired buggy. He handed her into the seat and walked around, throwing another look at Amanda still watching from the porch. He touched his hat brim to her as he crossed behind the buggy. Amanda waved gaily.

Beside him in the seat, the flower from the office desert looked even better in night bloom, prettily dressed and subtly perfumed. A sidewise inventory of her collided with one of

49

the same she was giving him. Her hands worked idly with the large red brocaded evening bag in her lap.

He turned the lazy dun down the first side road he came to, away from the town. Ann relaxed in her corner. A rind of moon rolled in the high white fluff of thunderheads, though the long twilight held on, and the dry skillet smell of greasewood floated from the cooling canyons. He walked the horse, continuing the random direction. The deserted lane led to the town's outskirts.

Abruptly, Ann made a small throaty laugh. 'This road! Do you know where it goes?'

There was such private, schoolgirlish merriment in her tone that he felt disconcerted. 'No . . .'

'But of course you wouldn't, a stranger.'

'Suppose you tell me.'

'To a place—' She paused as if belatedly embarrassed. 'We call it Hooligan's Corral. It's an old abandoned cowpen and tumbled-down barn with—with old bunks still in it, down at the end of the road in the cedar roughs.' As if that needed more explanation, she added matter-of-factly, 'It has a reputation. I mean— nice girls don't go there.'

He chuckled. If there had been any ice, she had smashed hell out of it.

'Maybe you underrate my knowledge of the local scenery. What if I said I'd known all along that Hooligan's Corral was down here?'

'But you couldn't have!' she exclaimed seriously. Then she laughed and the ice was further broken. He found himself liking her laugh, which was spontaneous, slightly husky, but maybe a trifle nervous.

'Do you ever come to Hooligan's Corral with your admirer, Son Hebron?'

Her retort was fast, and freezing with her sarcasm. 'Why surely, almost every night, Mr. Scott.'

'I'm Vic—let's make it Vic and Ann. And I shouldn't have implied what I did.' He added, 'Maybe it was this hired horse that took this direction, just from habit.'

'No harm done. You might turn around here, though, and take the crossroad to the courthouse.'

As he sawed the buggy about for the turn, Ann looked straight ahead with a slight frown, as if none of this was worth the candle. She was already disappointed in the evening, he thought.

He decided to try another tack. 'Your landlady seems pleasant, and quite a looker. Have you roomed at Amanda's for some time?' *Ever know Amanda's friend, Drew Cooper, murdered in the Bitter Creek roughs?*

'Are you interested in Amanda? My goodness, what has become of all the feminine charm I used to think I had?'

Once again her guileless directness made match-sticks of the courtroom poise he had

51

fancied he possessed; you had to knock off any wool-gathering to cope with this witness.

'I'm interested in you. For instance, how a woman as attractive and intelligent as you are would waste her charms on the town bad boy. There must be more eligible men, even in Angelo.'

She did not rise to the bait. From a far-off place she said musingly, 'You know, I'm still puzzled why I am here with you. I don't go out with just any hotel guest who asks me—'

'You wanted to flaunt your female independence before Son Hebron. So you used me.'

He sensed her small shrug. 'No . . . I think it was just because I was homesick. I've been out here only six months. It can get lonesome.'

'Homesick? Where is your home?'

'You wrote it in the register. That's what decided me, I guess.'

'I wrote it—?'

'Fort Worth.'

Damned if she wasn't full of surprises. He would have to play this cautiously. Could be a deliberate trap.

'So you saw Fort Worth in the register and it made you homesick. Am I the first visitor in Angelo from that city?'

'There have been others.'

'Did you date them, too? So you could stir up Son's jealousy? You know I'm risking trouble with him, don't you? Taking you to the dance?'

She still spoke from far away. 'Tell me about Fort Worth, Vic—who do you know there?'

He tensed, not liking this. Too much of a coincidence? Was she following someone's instructions?

'Well, the old town's about the same. My work keeps me out in the range country, mostly. Been up in the North Plains and Panhandle these last few years—'

She came alive. '*Where* in the Panhandle?'

'Oh, around Amarillo, and across in Indian Territory—' *Now don't ask me what Indian chiefs I know.*

'Amarillo!' She stirred and impulsively touched his arm, bending forward to peer delightedly up into his face. 'Vic! I was *born* in Amarillo! We lived there before we moved to Fort Worth. Mercy, isn't it odd how we—?'

'Oddest thing I ever heard of.'

She made him talk of Fort Worth and Amarillo. He faked it out. She seemed not to care too much about his answers—she was remembering, speaking animatedly of old times as if recounting small girlish trinkets left over from better years. He told himself, *She's sure-enough homesick for civilization or she's the best actress that anybody ever sent to trail me.*

When he had the opening, he said, 'Biggest news when I was leaving Fort Worth the other day was the escape of Prez Duvall. The town was all stirred up over it.'

53

Alertly listening, he caught her momentary hesitation. Her pleasure drained out and something else came into her voice. 'Oh, yes. Everyone talked about it here. They all knew Prez. One of our more notorious citizens.'

'I suppose Sheriff Moon is on the constant lookout for signs of him.'

'I suppose. But Arch Moon is not exactly a relentless manhunter.'

'Some were claiming the Hebron bunch or some of Prez's kin from out here helped pull the escape. Murdering those guards wouldn't bother a bunch of bandits much. Saved Prez from hanging.'

'Well, I suppose it's possible that old Felix would be barely smart enough to plan it. He's just a liquor-drinking, born-mean old cattle thief, actually, and his brother, Judge Ed, isn't much better.'

'Then nephew Son,' he said quickly, 'must be a great improvement over the rest of the clan.'

She said distantly, 'You're about to do some business with the Hebrons. On the shady side, too, I'd hazard. So maybe *they* can tell you all about Prez.'

'Shady? What gives you the idea?'

'You gave it to Charlie, the clerk, yourself. How else would a buyer deal with the Hebrons?'

Cautiously, he made a final cast. Too crudely, he was afraid; but a last effort to avoid a complete water haul with this unpredictable

54

woman. 'I suppose if Prez was holed up around here somewhere, the gossip would have leaked out by now. At least to the people friendly to the Hebron crowd. And since you hear everything at the hotel, you'd have heard rumors about that.'

Expectantly, he waited.

Then, very distantly, Ann murmured, 'In the moonlight . . . on a buggy ride . . . me in my best dress . . . I can think of nothing more romantic, Vic, than to talk about Prez Duvall. Just *why* did we both waste an evening, I wonder . . .?'

All right, A.G., you take her over—she's too damn tricky for a mere sergeant to rope.

He retorted, 'A stranger in town isn't apt to work too fast with Son Hebron's girl. I'll see if I can make it up to you, though, on our way home.'

'No. You'd best keep Miss Ellen Johnston in mind.'

He thought the floor had fallen out of the buggy and himself with it. 'Ellen Johnston! What do you know about—?'

'A letter came for you tonight. Thick and prettily scented. With her name and an Austin address on it. I should have put it in your box— but by then you had asked me to the dance so I just violated the rules and probably the U.S. mail laws by holding it out on you until after tonight. A foolish whim, of course. My cowardly way of dealing with distant competition. You'll have it first thing in the morning.'

She cut a sly glance up at him. 'Is she pretty, Vic? And jealous?'

Disconcerted, he muttered, 'Very. To both questions.' He had confided in Ellen his destination but not the details of his mission, after her faithful promise not to write under any circumstances.

Briskly, Ann said, 'Turn here. That road will bring us in by the courthouse. We've already missed the first few dances, and probably the first two or three fist fights outside, to say nothing of Amanda watching all the doors for the tall new cattle buyer from the city . . .'

His edginess took over his judgment. Without intending it, not even thinking, he dropped the reins, twisted to her, took both her shoulders in his strong fingers. He brought her face very close. 'You listen to me, Ann Lindsay—you got up on the wrong side of the bed, or you didn't take the chip off your shoulder when you put on that pretty dress— and I'm not thinking of Amanda Forester or some girl back east or what *you* think about crooked cattle buyers or—'

'Vic—you're holding me too—'

'All I know is you look good to me with that white moonlight on you and you have accused me of a blind side to romance, and now as one old Amarillo neighbor to another I aim to kiss you here and now—'

He did. Once started, he turned it into more than he intended, not knowing when to stop, or

56

where, or wanting to. She made no struggle, no regretful sigh afterward, but smoothed her dress and drew to her side of the seat. He took up the reins with hands trembling and headed the rig for the hitching places on the courthouse grounds. He steeled himself for the expected flare of outrage, or the stagy humiliation of the woman violated. Instead, she looked straight ahead and spoke as calmly as if remarking that it was a pretty night.

'A kiss is more romantic when the girl isn't being crushed against a shoulder holster and gun.'

In the tree shadows he saw the glow of cigarettes where the inevitable knot of outside hangers-on collected to pass the bottle. One called, 'Hey, bring your girl over here, friend— we'll warm 'er up for you.'

Vic muttered, 'Always at least one trouble spot outside a dance.'

'Pay no attention, Vic.' She firmly caught his arm and steered him among the buggies to the entrance. There, another small knot of men lounged. Sounds of fiddle music came from the windows, with the scraping shuffle of many feet on cornmeal-powdered floor. A large bulk of a man detached himself from the group and Vic was confronted by Son Hebron. Light from the vestibule lamps revealed his angered features. Vic smelled Son's whisky and knew that here was trouble.

'Been lookin' for you,' Son said accusingly to

Ann. 'I'm havin' the first dance—'

Ann's fingers tightened on Vic's forearm. He pulled free from her and stepped between them. With a short, abrupt motion he placed his palm flat against Son's chest and thrust him into a backward stumble. Son flailed at the men who caught and balanced him.

'I got to whup this city sonofabitch—'

Ann said sharply, 'Son—!'

Another man, even larger than Son, powered through.

Sheriff Arch Moon said firmly, 'There'll be no trouble in front of a lady. Now *vamoose*, all of you—'

One of the group let out a high, mocking *yipeee-e-e* yell. A laugh rippled through. Arch Moon grinned good-naturedly but kept blocking Son. Ann was determinedly pulling Vic toward the door.

'They're more bark than bite,' she said hurriedly. 'Son was just trying to show off. I'll give him a dance later and everything will be all right.'

He doubted that. Gloomily, he thought that he and Son Hebron must have been preordained to have trouble the minute he hit this town. Funny how fate could be like that. Sometimes a man had a ready-made enemy waiting somewhere ahead in his life. To run into him eventually shouldn't be surprising. What made it baffling was that it should be over this particular girl. A puzzling, old-young

58

woman, who would speak of romance and moonlight and Hooligan's Corral and could identify a shoulder gun by the feel of it even in the middle of a long crushing kiss and who knew more about Prez Duvall than she thought she had exposed to Vic.

But identifying a hidden gun could work both ways. In that heady moment of the long kiss in the buggy, she had dropped her red evening bag from her lap. When he had retrieved it for her afterward, his fingers had closed upon the familiar feel of a hard, small object within. During the seconds when he had clutched it, he knew that this was the outline of a small revolver. Ann Lindsay, it appeared, had come armed for the evening, with a wicked little derringer inside her frilly brocaded bag.

A woman's standard equipment out here? Or something just for him?

The impact of bright lights, shrill music, and milling dancers struck him all together as Ann turned tentatively and looked up to search his thoughts. As he put his arm about her, she favored him with a rare, surrendering smile. They glided into the dance stream just as Vic looked over her shoulder. Son Hebron was watching from outside a low window. Beside Son was his Coyote Face friend and one of the Hebron riders Vic had seen in the saloon. And beyond them, moving across the dim patch of light, he saw the tall, angular form of Captain Kincaid.

CHAPTER SEVEN

In the first few minutes he decided two things: Ann danced as lightly as a wisp of silk and enjoyed it; but she was studying him, appraising him, listening to him, with more than ordinary polite attention of a local girl to a new man.

Amanda Forester pushed through the jam of perspiring dancers and found them at an intermission. She chatted vivaciously, and reminded Ann that she was entitled to a dance with the man from Fort Worth.

In a small lull, Ann pointed out to Vic a man in the line-up of spectators in chairs at the rear of the hall.

'That's Judge Ed Hebron, Felix's brother. Son stays with him most of the time when he isn't at the ranch. Ed's an old bachelor.'

Amanda commented bluntly, 'Ed's a smelly old stallion, or worse. He sits out the dances because no woman in her right mind would allow him within six feet of her.'

Vic glimpsed the judge, a raw-boned, unshaven man of about sixty, shabby in suspenders and collarless shirt, who watched the scene with watery red eyes and talked sourly with a cluster of his cronies.

A town merchant was present to claim Ann when the music started up again, and Vic danced into the crowd with Amanda.

'Do you know what everyone is talking about?' Amanda whispered. 'They're glad to see Son Hebron have a little competition.'

'That so?'

'You might remember that he's a jealous fool. Any Hebron is meaner inside than he looks outside, which is plenty.'

'Is Ann seriously interested in him?'

He felt her shrug. 'She should be able to do better than that. But she's been going with Son ever since she came here. Ann is a little hard to understand.'

'She thinks highly of you, Mrs. Forester.'

'Amanda,' she corrected. She tilted her dark curls and gave Vic a full look. 'I'm divorced, you know, even if everyone still calls me Amanda Forester.'

'I met Tully today. Hope to make a cattle deal with him.'

'If you can deal with the Hebron bunch you're a better man than I am. I tried it for five years, living with Tully and those hyenas. Not that I hold any grudge against Tully. Except one.'

'And what was that?' *Does it have to do with the murder of Drew Cooper?*

Amanda noticeably tightened her hand on him but did not reply. Vic said casually, 'They seem to be an unduly suspicious bunch.'

'Of course. That's Felix and Ed—you would have to know their history out here. It's the way they grew up. Any stranger is an enemy until proved otherwise.'

The noise and jostling made talk difficult.

61

He felt that there was information in the offing tonight: from this woman who had been Tully's wife and Cooper's friend; and from Ann Lindsay, whom he could not yet classify. But tauntingly, the means of getting at it seemed just beyond reach. There was only so far he could go without exposing himself as too curious.

The night wore on. Once he saw Son Hebron bent over in a low talk with Judge Ed. Later, Son had disappeared. He searched over the crowd and found that Ann had disappeared, too. A nibble of worry ate along his spine.

He found Amanda again at an intermission. 'Been looking for you. I've seen them all and I've decided who's the most attractive woman in Angelo.'

She tilted her dark curls again, and her red lips and spirited black eyes smiled together in appreciation. 'I'm a good cook, too.'

'Well, I'd like to arrange for my evening meals at your place, here and now. Can you take another boarder? Daytimes I'll probably be out on the range.'

'Gladly. It will give us a chance to become better acquainted—Vic.'

He smiled and murmured, 'I hope so, Amanda.'

She looked about suddenly and said, 'Where's Ann? Are you already the jilted suitor?'

'Evidently. She seems to have disappeared.

Would you care to go out for a bit of fresh air and a better chance for us to talk?'

She looked up to study him, lightly running the tip of her tongue along her lips. He saw the affirmative decision forming. Then, a fuzzy-cheeked youth in a too-tight suit worked through to them. 'Mister, somebody wants to see you out front a minute.'

'That's a put-up job, Dink Mills!' said Amanda harshly. 'Vic, don't go. It'll be some fool country trick they'll pull on a stranger.'

'No, it's important,' Dink insisted. 'Lady out there wants him—'

Vic's mind leaped to the assumption that Ann had sent for him. 'Excuse me.' He escorted Amanda to a chair and left her, heedless of her protests. He shouldered through to the lighted hallway and the double doors. He walked to the faintly illuminated yard just beyond the entrance.

A small knot of loiterers waited there.

A man moved up and blocked his way. 'The city feller. You want to have a little snort with us, mister? Always glad to accommodate a stranger in town.'

One of them laughed. 'Come on around the corner, big boy. Have a drink with friends.'

'He's lookin' for his girl—'

'She jilted you, big boy—'

'Shut up, Red—'

Vic said, 'No thanks, I just—'

All at once there were too many around him,

63

closing in. Damn it, was there no way to avoid a ruckus with these toughs? Was it merely the standard rawhide for a city visitor, or something more vicious, set up by Son?

All at once the sheer force of them propelled him ahead and around the corner. As he tried to turn and face them, he heard a triumphant oath. Directly in his path loomed the coyote-faced chum of Son Hebron's.

Real alarm triggered over Vic. There was no playful hazing in Coyote's intentions.

Coyote's arm was extended back, and now it flashed upward and around, beginning the downswing of a bottle.

As he tried to dodge the blow, Vic was shoved by unseen hands at his back. The bottle swung by Coyote smashed a glancing blow across his temple. Staggered by pain, Vic crumpled to his knees.

Someone cautioned, 'Enough of that, Coyote—'

'No, it ain't!'

Coyote balanced, hoisted the bottle again, and Vic scrambled in desperation for Coyote's legs. His tackle brought Coyote threshing down upon him, and then there was a crazy, flailing mix-up on the ground. The others dodged about above the tangle of the two fighting men. Vic swung a savage punch upward, and the hot pain pleased him as his knuckles caught Coyote's eye socket. Coyote fell aside, fought to his feet, and retreated to the edge of light at the corner. Vic flung two men out of his path and went for him.

Backing up, Coyote smashed the bottom of the quart bottle against the stone wall.

'Now, damn you!'

Coyote waved the jaggedly broken bottle by its neck. Someone called hoarsely, 'No—don't do it—!'

The protest got lost in the ringing in Vic's ears as he weaved and feinted, the blood of fear washing against the pain in his head. He tried to keep his hazy vision on the snakelike darting of the glistening teeth of the broken bottle.

A tall shadow materialized back of Coyote, crowding up to him.

'Now, you boys—oughtn't to haze the feller so rough.'

It was enough to cause Coyote to hesitate. Then, Captain Kincaid's arm made a fast reach, Coyote's wrist snapped, the jagged bottle fell, and Kincaid's wide-open palm slapped Coyote reeling to the ground like a child.

Captain Kincaid turned, slipped Vic a wink, dusted his hands and called, 'You boys behave, now. Let's move around yonder and have a drink before Arch Moon comes and lights into us.'

Kincaid trudged around the corner. Someone asked awesomely, 'Who is that old codger?'

Another said to Vic, 'Just a little hurrah, mister. We didn't know Coyote was goin' to get

65

mean—'

They trailed around the corner behind Kincaid.

Vic had seen cowtown country-dance hurrah before. Coyote had meant this to be something different. The broken bottle could have shredded a man's face to bloody ribbons. But the first fact was, Coyote had meant to knock him out.

Son's instructions?

He made his way toward the dark trees where he had hitched the horse and buggy. He failed to see them and numbly stopped, wondering if he was groggy and had lost his bearings. He dabbed at his temple where the blood oozed.

He saw movement in the trees, but the figure who appeared there kept a discreet distance.

'The old feller who knocked down Coyote,' the voice guardedly began, and Vic recognized it as Canary Lenny's, 'he said tell you Son Hebron run off with your girl. In your buggy.'

'Where would they have gone?'

The shadow snickered. 'Most times, couples slippin' off from a dance head for Hooligan's Corral to do their courtin'.'

'Canary—wait a moment!'

But Canary back-tracked into the trees and was gone.

Vic started across the space where the buggy had stood. His foot struck something on the ground.

Stooping, he picked up Ann Lindsay's brocaded evening bag from the trampled broomweeds. His fingers closed on the outlines of the derringer inside. Thoughtfully, he brushed off the dirt.

He pushed the bag down into his coat pocket and walked quietly to the saddle horses tied among the mesquites. He selected a horse at random, led it into the more distant shadows, and mounted.

She had dropped her bag and had not retrieved it. If she had not been struggling with Son, then why hadn't one of them picked it up?

Aimlessly, at first, he let the horse take its own way along an empty lane. Then, remembering, he rode on with purpose. This was the road that led to Hooligan's Corral.

After a time he passed the place where he had turned the buggy at Ann's request, recognizing the spot in the starlight. The end of the road and the old barn in the cedar canyon wouldn't be far ahead. Vic pulled up and considered.

'Could be a wild-goose chase,' he cautioned himself. The problem gnawed again, whether he was butting into something that had shaped up long before his coming to town. He thought morosely that if he was smart he would leave Ann Lindsay and Son Hebron to their own devices.

The horse began pumping its neck and side-stepping. Stiffening, Vic strained to see in the

67

darkness.

Somewhere ahead he heard a rustle of sound, undefinable. He dismounted and led the horse off the trail that descended into the cedar-choked ravine. He saw below the faint outlines of the old barn and sagging rails of the pen. He kept to cover and worked on afoot.

An animal-like flurry of movement sounded somewhere downgrade. The brush crackled, then all was still again. Vic touched the butt of the small gun under his coat, loosening it. He pushed deeper into the cedars. Now the sounds were repeated. Human sounds, something told him. Then he heard the human moan, or a stifled sob, and a renewed scrambling in the cedars below.

Noiselessly, he worked his way down, already afraid of what he would find.

Ann Lindsay came out of the brush into his vision, falling once, clambering on the steep slope like a wounded thing, standing and trying again to run. Her hair stringed about her shoulders. Her party dress was torn and half hanging about her waist. She fought her way upward, crawling when she fell, struggling up again, and he heard her sobbing. Heedless of the noise, he plunged toward her, softly calling her name.

'Vic! Vic!' she cried, and clung wildly to him.

'Easy now. Just hold on a minute—'

She buried her face into him. 'Vic! He—Son

68

Hebron—'

Brutally, because he knew and, knowing, wanted to kill, he demanded, 'Is he still down there?' His arm tightened about her as he tried to see into the dark brush below. Her muffled voice came in a renewed seizure of fear.

'He's in there, somewhere, trying to find me. He went—crazy drunk, and I had to fight him—'

Now he heard the new shuffling coming through the brush below, the mixture of Son's hard breathing and mumbled cursing. Vic swung Ann away from him and upward on the path.

Son Hebron lumbered out from the brush like a grizzly, swaying and fighting the clutch of the bushes. The light revealed them to one another. Son kept coming, growling under his breath, and the starlight played a gleam on the sixgun raised in his hand.

Vic gritted to Ann, 'Keep going! Fast, now!'

'He'll try to kill you! Watch him, Vic—'

Son snarled across the low brush, 'Buttin' in on me again—!' Wildly, he extended his gun and the night split with flame and explosion. The slug of death fanned across Vic's right shoulder, splitting the fabric, searing a line of bloody fire across his flesh. Then he knew with forlorn certainty that he faced a crazed beast and was going to have to kill or be killed.

Son staggered on, closing the distance, and once more he fired wildly at the man a dozen

69

paces upgrade. The bullet chopped out a shower of cedar twigs. Son stopped and stood swaying, his features contorted, his hair tangled, squinting, trying to level for a point-blank aim.

Vic's little revolver seemed to perform of its own accord. His finger had only to brush the trigger. The crack was a childish sound after the sixgun's giant roar. One shot—and a black spot momentarily showed itself in Son's forehead. The towering mass of him stretched high on tiptoes for a second. Then Son sank noiselessly out of vision into the cover of the cedar.

Wheeling, Vic struggled up the path. He caught up with Ann who fiercely grasped his arm and stared wild-eyed. He saw the bruise on her cheek, her tangled hair; her partial nakedness momentarily forgotten.

'Did you—is he—dead?'

'He's dead.'

She clung to him for a moment, then seemed to steady herself. 'Are you hurt?'

'I'm all right. Quick, now, before somebody comes.'

They found the buggy and Vic whipped the horse to a trot toward the dark town. Ann huddled in her corner, working her hair out of her face, trying to fasten the remnants of her bodice at her breast.

'I thought I could handle him. But he—turned into an animal.'

70

'Why didn't you yell when he dragged you off? Couldn't you have called out for help?'

'At first he said he just wanted to talk to me about something. I—I just couldn't start yelling, with all those toughs out there—that my—my fellow was forcing me into the buggy. I still thought I could handle him. He was never like that before—then, finally—back there—I fought him till I could break away ...'

The tears came again, but she tried to control herself, and Vic groped for her hand. *Son Hebron dead.* Here was trouble compounded. The whole mission tottered in the balance tonight. His own alibi had to be fixed, and exactly right. Everything depended on this girl. He had to bring some semblance of a plan out of the jumbled turn of affairs, and he had to talk sense to her. Fast.

'You are to say nothing to anyone. I don't know whether you're a friend of all the Hebrons or not—surely not Son's, after tonight. Either way, remember that you were in on what happened to Son. You'd better get ready to lie with all the talent you've got.' He repeated the warning, harshly. 'Whatever involves me will involve you. Now, tomorrow— or whenever they question you—nothing happened, remember. You don't know anything. You were driven home by Son and that's the last you saw of him. He just drove you home in my buggy, because you got angry with me at the dance over something—make it over

71

Amanda. You got out and went to your room and that's the last you ever saw of Son. Can you make that stick?'

She had been trying to cut in. 'I'm *not* a friend of the Hebrons! If my bag had been with me, I would have done to Son what you did with your little gun—'

'All right. I trust you. Now—Sheriff Moon will soon know that a small caliber gun did it. Means I've got to get rid of this shoulder rig. But I'll handle that.' He halted the buggy behind the still darkened house of Amanda Forester. 'Do you trust Amanda?'

'I don't know. Maybe . . .'

Vic exploded. 'Good God, Ann! What's all the mystery about you? You've been going with Son, you seemed to hit here with your cap set to catch him! Why that little derringer in your bag? Why all the evasions?'

'Vic, please. My brain hurts and my body hurts all over. I don't want to talk.'

He helped her from the buggy and she led him to the side door, the private entrance to her room in the back wing of Amanda's house.

He said, 'Don't light a lamp when you get inside. Hide these clothes until you can burn them. If anybody comes to question you, try to make them talk through a window. Maybe you'd better stay in tomorrow—say the tragedy has upset you, you don't feel like going to work.'

She pressed her head against him. 'Vic! I see

72

him still—the way he was tearing at me—Now he's back there—dead—'

He gently brushed back her hair, feeling her trembling. 'I'm sorry it had to be this way. The next few days won't be easy. I'd best get moving, now—'

He waited until he heard her lock the door from inside. Far off, horses were on the gallop. He hurried to the buggy and drove away from the town. He abandoned the buggy and horse on the deserted road and walked back. He took to the dark alleys until he reached the rear of the wagon yard. He tossed a small rock upward into the open window, waited, and threw another. A shadow moved, well back inside the room. Removing his boots, Vic slipped up the back stairway.

Captain Kincaid had his door opened a crack and a Colt in his hand. Vic told the story, tersely. The old man grunted once, 'Godamighty!' but he heard Vic out without censure and said, finally, 'All right, Vic. A thing will happen. What next?'

'I want to get to my room. Ahead of Sheriff Moon, if possible. My story is, somebody took my buggy and I walked. My girl ran off and left me. This cut across the shoulder I'll claim I got from Coyote in the fight. This shoulder gun's got to be disposed of, so it'll never be found. I don't want to just junk it in an alley—too much risk.' Vic paced up and down in his stocking feet. 'Suppose—suppose you wrapped it in a package first thing in the morning and dropped it in the post office, addressed to Paul and Co. That'll get it out of both our hands—and the agent will know the meaning and how to get rid of it.'

He could sense Kincaid considering this, in the dark.

'I'll do it. Nothing better occurs to me. Now, if they put pressure on you, I'll be in a position to start a few rumors on some other suspect. Maybe this Canary Lenny—anybody to throw 'em off the scent. I'll be in touch . . . One thing, I picked this up by hanging around with the boys tonight, doing a lot of listening—while you was inside, fandangoing.'

When he paused, Vic asked brusquely, 'What's that, Captain?'

'The veterinarian and Son had been off somewhere together. That suggest anything? And Son set up Coyote to knock you out when the toughs started the hurrah.'

Vic grunted acknowledgment, then whispered of his need for haste and got out, pulling on his boots again and hurrying down an alley. Somewhere he heard riders pull up on the street, exchange words, and caught the name, 'Son Hebron.' So the shooting was known, the chase started. He came to the Lehman House from the rear, found the yard gate locked, and scaled the board fence. He went up the back stairs, cursing the squeaking boards, and into the dark hall-way.

74

He reached his door and saw the thin crack of light showing beneath the door.

So he was too late.

Sheriff Arch Moon sat on his bed, his slumbering stare narrowed and waiting, his .44 out and loosely held.

Vic turned his back and closed the door. In that first glimpse, he knew, Moon had seen the bruise on his temple and the bloody rip across his coat. Vic faced back to the unmoving giant.

'What's the trouble, Sheriff?'

'There's been a killing.'

'So I heard. Too bad.'

Vic stood in uncertainty. Some of the slumber went out of Moon's expression.

'How'd you get that coat rip? Looks like blood.'

'I had a fight at the dance. Those toughs jumped me.'

Moon nodded slowly. 'Heard about that. You happen to carry a little gun on you? Twenty-five caliber maybe?'

'Happen not. Why?'

'I'll search you. But there's a hundred places you could have dumped it.'

Vic submitted to the big hands in silence. His valise, he saw, and the drawers already had been ransacked. As Moon finished, the door swung open behind Vic. Deputy Sam Tabor came in and stood tall and unspeaking.

Moon shook his head. 'He ain't packin' any iron.'

Tabor said, 'I've got men looking for Canary Lenny.'

'You see the girl?'

'She was in bed. Just talked to her through a window. Son took her home early, then drove off. In this fellow's buggy. That's all she knows.'

Moon considered. 'The Hebrons wouldn't want us to overlook anything.' To Vic he said mildly, 'I'm gonna take you over to the jail for the night, Scott. Just playin' safe. I don't want to stump my toe on this case.'

Vic went through the expected protests, but the outcome was the same. After a while he stood in a cell in the squat stone jail at the rear of the courthouse, hearing the cell door slam shut, seeing Sheriff Moon working the key. Moon muttered, 'G'night,' and returned to the front office.

Vic heard the sheriff say something, and Deputy Tabor's voice. Then Moon said audibly, 'Nothing for me to do, Sam, but send you out for old Felix. He would want to know about this.'

Vic sank to the iron bunk, weak from the burn in his shoulder and the renewed surge of pain in his head. One thing seemed certain. Before the morning was very old, he was going to meet Felix Hebron in the flesh. Right through the bars of this cell door. While the notorious Felix looked him over like an animal in a cage.

CHAPTER EIGHT

The cell door squeaked open and Sheriff Moon called, 'Scott! Get up and come on out here!'

Vic winced first against the burn in his shoulder wound as he sat up, then against the sun glaring through the barred window. He groped for his clothes, and remembrance of the night came back to him in bitter fragments. Now, he supposed, Felix Hebron was going to sit like a jury and decide what was to be done.

Moon waited silently until Vic was ready, then motioned him to follow down the corridor. Moon sat uneasily at his office table and Vic took the opposite chair and waited. He checked back over the pattern of his alibi and decided that it was as full of holes as a prairie-dog town.

'You waiting for Felix Hebron, Sheriff?'

'Him and Tully Forester are out at the hitch rack, talkin'.'

'While they talk, I've had no coffee, no breakfast, and I need a doctor to disinfect this knife cut in my shoulder. Who's your jail doctor?'

It didn't get anywhere. Moon only shifted his weight and looked blank.

'Sheriff, it ought to be plain to you I had nothing to do with whatever happened to Son Hebron. I had no cause—only knew him by sight.'

'Felix will decide.'

'Was he right fond of his nephew?'

'He ain't right fond of anybody. But the Hebrons won't stand for something like that without takin' care of it.'

'What's done to the least of them, it's done to Felix, eh? Like in the Scriptures.'

'How's that?'

'Never mind.'

Whatever Moon and his cagey deputy, Sam Tabor, might have uncovered during the night was going to stay locked behind that puffy blankness. Vic would be left to dangle until the moment they were ready to spring some triumphant discovery and trap him.

Two men came from the dusty sunlight and Vic turned for his first look at Felix Hebron. He was surprised to see a graying man of nondescript shabbiness, a patch of untended stickery chin whiskers, shapeless pants and scuffed boots. In his first reaction, Vic was reminded of a slovenly East Texas backwoodsman, except for Felix's sun-fried color and his jerky, muscular movements indicating perpetual itch to get a thing done. His mouth drooped in a false smile, made by a drawn lip corner. He crossed to a chair near Moon, while his washed-out eyes lashed a sour appraisal between the sheriff and Vic Scott. Tully Forester closed the front door, plunging the office into shadows again.

Instead of leaning back, Hebron leaned forward and nervously worked at hooking each

78

thumb into his belt. His black vest gaped open and his faded flannel shirt and wrinkled neck looked to be a few days past washing. His fixed mouth-corner droop exposed the crest of a tarnished gold tooth. Vic recalled Ann Lindsay's description: *A liquor-drinking, born-mean old cattle thief.*

The man was more than that. Vic sensed the kingpin's crafty assurance, the peculiar inner force of a warped arrogance which had built itself within Felix on that long and violent road from small-time brush rustler to top dog in the isolated county.

Felix made a detailed visual examination of Vic, then of Moon, as if assessing the worth of low-grade cattle. His jaw knots stood out. Tully chewed his cigar and looked at his hands.

Felix's voice came out raspy thin. 'Is this him, Arch?'

'Yeah. Victor Scott. Cattle buyer from Fort Worth.'

'Well? What about it, Arch? He kill the boy?'

Moon gazed at his table top.

Felix's scowl deepened. 'You got the goods on him, Arch? You ready for my boys to take over?'

Moon muttered, 'How you mean, take over?'

'Why, you could release him to us, Arch. We would take him on a little trip.'

'I don't know,' the sheriff said bleakly. 'We

79

just don't know what happened. I thought you-all would want to talk to this feller.'

Felix jerked in exasperation. 'You had all night and you still don't know who killed my nephew?'

'Felix, we been workin'—'

Felix snapped a short obscenity of contempt.

Moon protested, 'We ain't had but a few hours—'

Felix shifted and thrust his wrinkled neck forward. 'Scott, did you murder my nephew?'

'Mr. Hebron, from what I've heard, Son wasn't worth the powder it took. Everybody knows you and Judge Ed have made good out here, gotten way up in the world—but Son was scrub stock and he wasn't worth a damn to either of you. You're just wasting our time when you and I could be doing some business.'

It wasn't the kind of denial they had expected. Tully shuffled his feet and Felix blinked.

'We ain't talkin' about what Son was worth. What I want to know is who murdered the boy in cold blood.'

'There must have been a hundred people around here who had one cause or another to dislike your nephew. I didn't even know him.'

'He was blood kin of ours. Whoever done him in has got me to answer to.'

'My only interest out here, Mr. Hebron, is to buy cattle.'

That diverted Felix slightly. His jaw marbles

80

worked in thought. 'We got some stuff for sale. Understand you're a man that likes a deal.'

'Buying cattle is my business. I like to make a trade, I like to make money. For myself, and for the other fellow.'

The gold tooth came back in sight. Felix scratched his chin stubble.

Tully Forester took the cigar out of his mouth. 'Now not so damned fast on this. Scott, you had a run-in with Son at the saloon and trouble of some kind at the dance.'

Vic shrugged. 'Nothing important, Tully.'

Felix turned shrewd again. 'It was over a girl, too. Ain't that right?'

Vic was ready for that. Here he would throw a left-handed loop and from an unexpected direction. 'Mrs. Forester has got nothing to do with it.' He laughed shortly. 'It's correct that I danced quite a few with her, and I did make arrangements to take my evening meals at her boarding house. But I didn't figure that would make any difference to Son. Or to you either, Tully. Amanda is a very attractive lady, and I say that in all respect.'

It took them a tedious half minute to sort out the kinks in their minds and get them straight. Having tossed them the red herring of Amanda Forester, Vic waited. He put on a puzzled, honest expression, as if wondering what Tully's ex-wife had to do with this.

Tully was the first to correct him. 'Not talking about Amanda. Talking about the one you took to the dance. The girl Son was sweet on.'

'Oh. The girl at the hotel.' Vic relaxed. 'Well, I guess after Amanda and I sort of hit it off, Miss Lindsay got riled and took out. I found she was not interested in anybody but Son, so I turned my attention to Amanda.'

It sounded reasonable, he hoped. It *had* to. He had to rub out the least trace of any motive for blasting the life out of Son Hebron at Hooligan's Corral. And if Ann Lindsay did not back him up, his neck was in a noose.

Felix said, almost forlornly, 'Ann is a fine girl. She'll be hard hit over this. I don't know what she saw in the boy, but I reckon he had a way with wimmin.'

Tully studied Vic closely. 'How'd you get that slice across your shoulder?'

'Some of your local toughs jumped me at the dance. The one with the coyote mug made a swing at me with a knife—'

'Coyote Thatcher,' Moon confirmed. 'They did have a scuffle.'

Felix sourly commented, 'Son loafed around town with trash like him when he ought've been puttin' in a day's work.'

Tully bored in again. 'Then Son went off with the girl you took. Ann Lindsay. In your hired buggy. You didn't try to find 'em?'

Time for another red herring. 'I ran across a fellow they call Canary—'

Felix grunted and whipped an accusing

82

glance at Tully.

'Lenny told me they had left the dance, so I went back and looked for Amanda. But I couldn't find her in the crowd, or else she had left.' He made a sour grin at Felix. 'So I finally hoofed it back to the hotel. After that little mix-up with Coyote, I'd had all of that party I wanted.'

Felix grunted at Tully. 'Canary Lenny, huh? He come back to town?'

'Yeah. Son told me—'

Moon said, 'Sam Tabor is lookin' for him.'

Felix snapped, 'Find him, damn it!' He added irritably, 'There's one thing after another.'

He let that go without amplifying his worry and Vic thought, *He means all this on top of Prez Duvall.* Inwardly, Vic allowed himself a small edge of relief. He had tossed before them his interest in Amanda, his complete unconcern for Son Hebron's girl, Ann Lindsay, and the name of Canary Lenny. It was the best he could do at the moment.

Felix asked Moon, 'This feller have any iron on him?'

'Colt forty-five wrapped up in a belt in his suitcase. Clean.'

'Son was shot once, small caliber. That right?'

'Looked to be.'

'Any tracks down there?'

Moon shook his head. 'It's all rocks and

83

brush. No tracks we could make out. We found out Son took Ann home, then he must have drove off to Hooligan's in this feller's buggy. Maybe to see what he could stir up. He was pretty drunk all evenin'. Just no tellin' who waylaid him down there.'

Felix had decided. He said to Tully, 'Get the boys out lookin' for Canary Lenny. Damn it, everybody sits on their rump and the bastard that did it gets clean away.'

Vic waited tensely. Tully said reluctantly, 'All right, Felix.'

'Now, Scott, you ready to look at the cattle I got to offer?'

'As soon as I can get something to eat, Mr. Hebron, and this shoulder cut doctored. Do you know a doctor I can get to attend to it?'

Felix asked Tully, 'Where would Flayhorn be?'

'Treating that sick mare, likely.'

Vic wondered if he'd heard a flinty edge of meaning in Tully's tone. Felix mumbled, 'Reckon so,' then, 'Flayhorn's a veterinary doctor, but he'll do as good as the others for what you've got. Other two don't like me and by God I don't like them.'

Tully, near the window, said, 'Here comes Ed.'

Vic had thought it was over. He had sold his bill of goods, wrapped it neatly, and tied it with tinsel of sincere innocence. Felix was about to pick up the purchase, and now, damn it, here

84

came Judge Ed. Within a minute after Ed's arrival, his fear was confirmed. It was going to be reopened, he would have to do it all over again. They had to satisfy the elder brother.

Ed Hebron turned his red-streaked eyes and crabbed expression to Vic and asked, 'Is this him? He the one?'

'Don't think so, Ed,' replied Felix. 'We want Canary Lenny. Scott, here, he's buyin' some stuff from us.'

Ed stalked about and said plaintively, 'Well, I wish you'd take care of another thing or two, before you go into *that*. I got my hands full enough. Then this thing has to happen to Son.'

'We'll find the man we want, Ed. Tabor's lookin' for him and Tully and some of my boys're going to be lookin' for him. What'd you know about last night?'

Judge Ed scowled. 'Saw him at the dance.' He jerked his chin at Vic. 'Dancin' with Amanda.' He stopped and planted his fingers in his hip pockets. 'What about him? What's he have to say?'

Felix gruffly began to tell it, but Ed insisted on asking Vic his own grouchy questions. They went through it again. Vic noticed that Tully listened intently in the background.

Finally, Ed said morosely, 'I got to arrange for the funeral, Felix. I just got more cussed things to look after than any of you—'

'When we going to have the funeral?'

'This evenin', I reckon. Get it over with.' Ed

85

shook his head dolefully. 'That poor girl, Ann—guess she'll be bad tore up about this. Figure she and Son would've got married, might of made something out of him. Well, if you think this feller is smellin' right, that's up to you. I'm leavin' that part up to you and your outfit, Felix.'

'We'll take care of it!' Felix retorted. 'Nobody's going to get away with anything. See you look after your own end—'

Judge Ed started to say something, seemed to think better of it, and stalked out, mumbling.

Felix followed, and they talked outside. Vic tried to hear their words, unable to show that he tried because Tully remained. Felix came back. 'Scott, you ride out to our Bitter Creek graze. Tully will show you what we got to sell.'

Vic said, 'All right. First, I'd like to get Doc Flayhorn to look at this shoulder.'

'Try his office. Tell him I sent you.'

'Thanks.'

'Arch, I want Canary Lenny found. Now get off your big rump and do something.'

Moon obeyed ponderously. 'I'll try, Felix. Canary is slippery, though.'

Vic stood and set his hat. They were awkwardly grouped, beginning a general move toward the door. Then Judge Ed turned back, bunching them up on one another. 'It's Amanda and Ann comin'—'

The two women entered together. His eyes met Ann Lindsay's and she immediately looked away, unsmiling. Amanda nodded, and then said, 'Hello, Tully.' Forester said, 'Amanda . . .' almost inaudibly, and Amanda turned and said, 'Hello, Mr. Scott.' The two women were freshly powdered, neatly dressed, a trifle sleepy, appropriately solemn.

Amanda addressed Felix. 'We want to know what we can do. Anything about the funeral, getting the preacher, and some ladies to sing—'

'Hadn't thought much about it,' Felix muttered. 'Reckon so. You want to work with Ed on it?'

Ann Lindsay moved nearer to Ed and looked coldly at Vic. 'Is he the one, Judge Ed?'

'They think not, honey.' Ann limply turned and placed her face against Ed's shoulder. He patted her and soothed, 'You poor little girl.' It touched them all. Felix promised hoarsely, 'You bear up, Ann—we gonna get the one that did it.'

'It's such a shock!'

Felix nodded glumly. 'Know how you feel. Thing like this is hard for a woman to have to endure. We were pullin' for you—think you could have made something out of the boy.'

Ann withdrew from Ed's sympathetic arm and turned away, touching a wadded handkerchief to her eyes.

Amanda watched it all with a cool smile. 'A woman's fate. We find our men and then we lose 'em.'

Ed said, 'You-all come on to my office and we'll get started on the funeral. Somebody's got to get out and drum it up.'

Amanda nodded and added, 'Else Son will play to an empty house.'

'By God they *better* be there!' Felix said impatiently. 'Pass the word in all the saloons, Arch. Tell 'em I said so—even if it's Son, he was a Hebron, and I want that church full.'

Ann walked to the door, her head down. Amanda spoke to Vic, 'I'll expect you to supper, Mr. Scott.' She added to Tully, 'You, too, Tully, if you're in town and want to.'

'Won't be here,' Tully said sharply. 'Got things to do after the funeral.'

Vic tried to digest what he had just witnessed: the cozy little scene of mutual sorrow. All he could make out of it was that Ann had been compelled to learn Vic's status this morning. And her own. That performance—real or faked? All the others had seemed to take it for granted that she and Son would eventually have been married. He wondered again if Ann had been put up to tricking him last night. And then had met her big trouble with her drunken suitor. Trouble not on her original program.

He walked alone toward the hotel. He watched the sidewalks ahead, after a glimpse at the empty window over the wagon yard office. The town was coming to life. A wagon stirred alkali dust on main street, horsemen were on

88

the move, a few pedestrians went their way along the plank sidewalks. In the second block he sighted the waiting figure he had hoped to see.

Captain Kincaid turned in the same direction Vic was walking and for a minute they were side by side. From the corner of his mouth Vic said, 'Get Canary Lenny to hide out, if he isn't already. Pronto.'

'He in trouble?'

'Lynch rope, likely, if they catch him. He knows something.'

'All right. You clear?'

'For the time being. Going to Doc Flayhorn's. Later, to the Hebron place. Felix wants to get rid of that stolen herd. They're all worried. They've damned sure got the one we want, somewhere.'

'I'm peddlin' it that Canary followed Son to where he was killed. Also invented talk about Coyote Thatcher, out of thin air. Just to sidetrack them for a while. Let me know how it smells out yonder. They got line shacks scattered to hell and gone—that's what I'll try to check out.' He added morosely, 'You sure ain't helped none.'

Kincaid drifted aside and turned into a hardware store, and Vic kept his course, bleakly aware of the truth in Kincaid's accusation.

He went to the hotel and called at the desk for mail. Charlie looked him over curiously and handed him a letter. Vic saw the familiar handwriting of Ellen Johnston and the Austin postmark.

In the room he cleaned up, hurriedly read the letter, then burned it in the wash bowl. He shredded the ashes and dusted them under the carpet. Ellen, she had said, just *had* to write to him in Angelo, despite her promise; she was sorry that she had been angry, and she still loved him—*love* underlined three times. *You keep writing me in Angelo, sweetheart, and you're likely to love me to death.*

He took out his Colt, examined its load, and buckled it on. A short time later he turned into the Angelo Café and took a back table, facing the entrance. The breakfast rush was long since over, and the day's pots of chili con carne and frijoles and ripe-smelling beef stew already were sending their odors from the kitchen. The thin waitress came with a tired smile and Vic said, 'Coffee right now, please, then ham, eggs over, biscuits . . .'

'Big excitement last night,' she said.

'Heard about it.'

'Yeah. Son finally got it. The one that did it, I would hate to be in his shoes.'

'They know who did it?'

'Sure. Canary Lenny.'

'What does Canary do?'

'Used to be a horse wrangler for the Hebrons. Been workin' south somewhere. I had a date with Son once, myself. I like a

90

different type, though, a nicer, more gentlemanly gentleman—'

'Well, I guess Sheriff Moon will solve it.'

She giggled shrilly and punched the pencil into her mounded-up red hair. 'Ain't that the *truth*!'

When Vic entered Doc Flayhorn's office from the outside stairway over a back-street saddle shop, the room was deserted. He closed the door, called out twice, then opened a door and investigated a second room. It was filled with a working counter, shelves, dusty bottles and cans, and the smell of liniments. Returning to the cluttered office room, he quietly pulled out the drawers in Flayhorn's roll-top desk. One held what he sought, a scruffed book dimly lettered *Accounts*. He hurriedly flipped through to where the entries carried recent dates and began to scan the scribbled notations.

An entry caught his eye: *Hebrons, sick mare, $5*. This carried a date, May 29. Vic counted back. His blood pumped hot as he fitted the time sequence. Assuming that it had taken four days of travel after Prez's bloody liberation, that's when he would have reached the Angelo country. He found three other entries, undated, charged to *Hebron* or merely *H, sick call, $5*. Altogether, there were five calls in eight days.

He murmured, 'That's a mighty sick mare.' Which Hebron? Somewhere on Felix's vast

91

range, or here in town, or at some remote Mexican shack, cared for by some member of the clan as yet unknown?

He was about to close the book and return it to the desk drawer when a small shower of papers fluttered out from its pages. They scattered to the floor in spite of his efforts to clutch them. Quickly, he got to his knees and began to collect the slips, seeing that they were scribbled notes of routine nature. He had almost finished when he heard the footsteps strike the bottom of the outside stairway and begin the ascent.

He crammed the loose notes into the book and thrust it into the open drawer. The steps outside neared the door as he worked at the drawer which turned cranky and stuck midway. Desperately, he jerked and sawed. It finally slid closed with a protesting scraping sound. He whirled and had almost reached a chair when the doorknob worked. A stooped, long-beaked man came in on a wave of medicine odors and yesterday's bar whisky.

Doc Flayhorn gave him a disinterested glance, a mumbled 'G' morning,' dropped his bag to the floor and hung his hat.

'Well, what's your trouble?' he grunted.

'I've got a shoulder wound, Doctor. I'd like for you to look at it.'

Vic's glance was signaled to the floor. Beneath Flayhorn's desk lay one overlooked scrap of folded white paper. The telltale slip seemed to shout its presence.

Flayhorn was wiping his spectacles. 'Shoulder wound?'

'Yes. From a little trouble last night. Knife slash. Felix Hebron said tell you he sent me.'

Flayhorn kept his preoccupied, unhappy expression. He told Vic to take off his coat and shirt. He made a close look at the raw red streak and mumbled, 'Knife, you say? Don't look like it.'

'What does it look like?'

Flayhorn began to take cotton and bottles from his bag.

'Looks more like a bullet to me.'

'Well, it could have been a broken bottle. It was quite a melee and I don't remember too well. Never heard any shot, though.'

'The drunks at the dance.' Flayhorn nodded. He soaked cotton from a smelly bottle. 'This'll burn. Heard about the trouble. You must be the cattle buyer. Steady, now.' Flayhorn questioned the cause of the wound no further. He stuck on a pad of bandage with salve and Vic worked back into his shirt. Flayhorn grunted and squatted before his desk. He reached and retrieved the folded paper. He opened it, glanced at the notation, then tossed it to his desk top. Vic saw him look toward the second desk drawer. The drawer was closed unevenly, with one edge sticking out.

'How much do I owe you, Doctor?'

'Generally get three dollars for an office call. Not licensed for this kind of thing. Just as soon you wouldn't talk about it.'

'I understand. Felix said you were as good or better than the others.'

Flayhorn scowled. He looked out the window. 'A snort of whisky might help us both. Too early to join me?'

'Be glad to.'

Flayhorn visibly brightened, as if a new friend had been found. 'That cut may pain you tonight,' he said, digging again into his bag. 'Here, this'll help.' He poured a few white tablets into his palm and extended them to Vic. 'Something new, called "sleepers." It's a pill that will put you to sleep.' As Vic thrust the loose tablets into his pants pocket, Flayhorn added morosely, 'When I've had a bad day, I use 'em myself.'

'Thanks. I've heard of sleepers. Never had any trouble on that score, though.'

'Trouble's all there is out here.' Then Flayhorn tried to brighten again as he went for a whisky bottle and glasses. He poured two generous drinks. 'Here's to you. Luck's what you'll need if you deal with the Hebrons.'

That's evident, Vic thought. *Whisky by day and sleeping pills at night.*

The Hebrons' sick mare was something to plague the doctor. He wondered if the whisky would loosen Flayhorn's tongue, if he could maneuver the talk to that subject.

CHAPTER NINE

The June sun hung like a hot skillet bottom from a handle of afternoon thunderheads, striking harsh reflections off the pock-marked adobe walls of Felix Hebron's headquarters house above Flint Creek canyon. A row of drooping chinaberry trees made weak puddles of shade along the low-roofed, junk-littered front porch. The untended yard stretched across to a distant bunkhouse and a cluster of corrals and sheds. The water tank, windmill, a few beanpole poplars and many eroded boulders filled the side yard. From there a dusty path led through the broomweeds a hundred yards to the three Mexican shacks.

Felix half dozed in his big chair on the front porch, sleepily seeing a Mexican walking across the far corral with an armful of hay. A stout, barefoot Mexican woman slumbered on a pallet at the side of one of the Mexican houses. Otherwise, the headquarters of the Hebron empire looked dead as a graveyard at that siesta time of day.

Behind Felix's chair, just inside the doorless opening to the dogtrot hallway, a Winchester rifle stood within arm's reach and a pair of binoculars hung from a nail above the rifle.

Neither the outside, with its shabby grounds, nor the interior indicated any recent clean-up efforts. Felix and Ed had always lived in bachelor untidiness; when Ed had moved to the house in town to be county judge he had only transferred his bachelor cave five miles south. As orphaned brothers, the two of them had sprouted from the wild land, as viciously self-sufficient as greasewood seedlings, and thereafter had lived close to the hot, thorny crust that spawned them.

Felix was disgruntled because he could only half take his siesta, and problems and worries of one kind and another had been stacking up recently. Now he was waiting for Tully Forester, and after a while he would have to retrace the hot road to town. Not only was so much unprofitable riding a nuisance; he also would have to endure the rigmarole of burying lazy Son. A lot of people would be looking at the Hebron crowd and people made him scratchy. The country was getting too crowded.

Not so long ago, if just one stranger came riding into the brush from either side of the Rio Grande, Felix and Ed and Tully would have known his size, age, purpose and armament hours before he reached Angelo settlement. Now they were all over the place, since the weekly stage service to Sweetwater, and with the railroad crew building the roadbed over which steel rails and trains would eventually follow. The only good thing he could see about it was that it should help the marketing of cattle. In recent years he had been cattle poor. The Hebrons always had their way in acquiring cattle and land because there was nothing in the remote region to stop them. Turning cattle into money was the problem. Increasingly, in recent years, it had been difficult to find anybody who would deal with the Hebrons.

The fellow, Victor Scott, from Stone & Chesman, could be a godsend, Felix speculated. It was a little peculiar that a big outfit like them would send a buyer out here to deal with him, because he knew his own reputation as well as the rest of Texas knew it. But the man had his own game, evidently, and Felix was ready to play it if he could turn, say, a thousand head. But one of the several things that kept itching his mind was that Scott had shown up right on the heels of that business with Prez.

Well, everybody, he guessed, was on edge over that. But they had their eyes open, they could spot a snooper, and they could take care of him. The last one who came out this far to stick his nose in, had been a slick sonofabitch, Felix thought, but they had taken care of *that* gentleman.

Tully Forester rode out of the first stand of mesquite and Felix awaited him in drowsy peevishness. Tully dismounted and came up the low steps, looking just as peevish, and wiped at his sweat and squatted to his boot heels against the porch wall. There was another chair, Felix thought grumpily, but Tully had to squat like a damned greaser.

He asked, 'Well, did you get some mourners

lined up?'

'Yeah. Alto is bringing some men from the Bitter Creek herd. No use to send to the Catclaws, that bunch couldn't make it in time. Lots of trouble, just for Son.'

'I know. He was trouble to the last. He hated work but he was a glutton for whisky and wimmin. He had to go take some filly down to that place, I reckon, and Canary Lenny waylaid him. But there's got to be a funeral audience. He was a Hebron. His dead pappy was my own brother.'

'I'm leaving Chock to watch the Bitter Creek trail for that cattle buyer. He's to keep him at the line camp till we get back. If it's too late, he can bunk there and I'll show him the cattle tomorrow. You satisfied about him, Felix?'

'I am if we can get rid of about a thousand head, including that Mexican stuff. I want to hit Scott for twenty dollars a round for a thousand head, and offer him a kickback of a dollar a round. We'll pretty damn soon settle whether he wants to do business.'

'All right. Everybody's got their eyes open. Where's Guiro? I'm starved.'

'Down at the pens while ago. Go fix you somethin'.'

Instead, Tully stood on the porch edge and whistled shrilly. In a moment, Guiro began the upgrade plod to the house. Tully squatted on his heels again, his back to the adobe. Guiro wiped his sleeve across his seamed face.

'What'd you want?'

'Something to eat. Get in the kitchen.'

Guiro mumbled protests and moved to the doorway. Felix stopped him. 'I haven't seen Leona around. Where is she?'

'She rode off on a mule before daylight.'

Felix cursed. 'She never asked me!'

Guiro shrugged and padded down the corridor. Tully remarked, 'You can just bet she slips off to see him.'

'I ought to break her leg. We're on enough dynamite without that.'

Tully gave him a malicious eying. 'Leona's lived on this place off and on as long as I can remember, but she's not worth a cow chip as a housekeeper. There must have been a time when she was good for something else.'

Felix kept his half-closed eyes tracing the far country. 'Could of been. When me and Ed first ran across her, Leona was young and juicy as a new pound of butter. Me and Ed were young, too, and we broke in with her. Godamighty, what a ruckus *that* caused!'

'She don't look appetizin' now.'

'Hell, man, none of us was more than sixteen-seventeen then. First time, we caught her by herself in a shack and took turns holdin' her for one another. It was like cuttin' a wildcat. You ought to know—ever' kid that ever grew up out here done it first with some line-camp Mex. Her husband was a greaser named Lauro and when he found out he

99

jumped Ed with a knife about two feet long and we shot him six times apiece. Buried him in some rocks somewhere in Cactus Grove, forgot where we did do it. Leona was always sproutin' seed, one might of been Ed's or mine for all we know. One could've even been Prez. I remember he grew up with a flock of Mexican kids. Blood gets all mixed up out here.'

Tully shifted uncomfortably and Felix noticed that. He grinned sourly. 'That scratch you? . . . Why don't you get up off your goddam heels and sit in a chair like something beside a greaser? Mex blood all run down to your feet, Chili?'

Tully stood and said heatedly, 'Don't call *me* Chili! Prez Duvall and Chock and Alto may be some of your washerwoman bastards but I'm not—'

'Oh, shut up, Tully. I'm just palaverin'. It don't make any difference.'

'Well, I don't like it . . . If you're going to that funeral, you'd better go shave and put on a clean shirt.'

'Got none,' Felix muttered. 'That damned Leona hasn't done a washing in two weeks.'

Tully stared off toward movement in the distance. 'I think that's her coming now.'

The figure of a woman materialized, with her skirts bunched up, straddling a mule. She attempted to turn the animal and circle behind the house. They saw that she carried a bundle balanced in front of her, and Felix sat up and

100

bellowed, '*Leona!* Come-mere!'

He muttered, 'I want to know where she's been.'

The Mexican woman reluctantly turned the mule toward the porch. Her graying black hair straggled from beneath her head shawl. She watched Felix from downcast slitted eyes in a creased, gaunt face.

'Where you been?'

'Just on a little ride,' she replied tonelessly in English.

'*Where*, damn you!'

'To see the Izaguirre woman at the camp. She's sick.'

'You're a liar! What's in the bundle?'

'Some of her clothes.'

'Open it!' Felix commanded. 'Get down and open it.'

Leona delayed a long time but Felix stood unrelenting, and she clumsily got down from the mule. Her bunched skirt fell back into place after revealing that was all she wore. Her sagging breasts made limp, unsupported mounds in the loose blouse. She placed the sheet-tied bundle on the bottom stoop and slowly began to untie it. Felix stood above her, waiting. Leona threw back the folds of cloth, exposing the laundry, and cocked her head up at Felix with her lips pulled in a defiant leer. 'So. Have your look.'

Felix bent and roughly pawed into the bundle.

101

'What I thought.' He glanced at Tully. 'Bloody bed sheets, a man's shirt, and bloody drawers. You lyin' old bitch. You had to go and see him.'

Leona muttered, 'They needed washing.'

'You found out and you went and no tellin' who saw you.'

She said simply, 'He's mine, Felix. He is my own. I was careful. Who would notice an old Mexican washerwoman—'

'Just every goddam body that might of been watchin', that's who!' Felix had turned red with his anger. She stooped and tied up the blood-stained bundle. Tiredly, she trudged up the steps past him and to the hall doorway. Felix turned with his mouth-corner scar drained white, and caught her just inside. He reached and locked his left forearm powerfully against her throat until she made gurgling breaths, and plunged his right hand into her blouse front. He found her sagging right breast and squeezed with crusty fingers. His thumb and forefinger worked to the nipple and he applied all the pressure of a steel vise. The woman stiffened convulsively; a moaning cry of pain burst through her clenched teeth. She struggled, but Felix held his grasp until it pleased him to release her. Then she snarled a sobbing curse, whirled, and groped wildly for the Winchester beside the doorway. Felix slapped her head half around, then pushed her with both hands into a stumbling fall to the

102

floor. 'You ask me next time, or I'll pinch it off.'

Guiro stuck his head out of the kitchen, then stoically helped Leona to her feet. Felix called back, 'You wash some clothes for *me* for a change, before you start on Prez's bloody stuff!'

Outside, he rejoined Tully who had taken it all in with his shoulder planted against a porch post. 'She's always threatenin' to go for a knife or a gun,' Felix said, 'but she's never had the guts to really do it.'

Tully turned back to watch the country. 'She'll use a knife some day when you're asleep. They don't ever forget what a gringo did to 'em, maybe twenty-thirty years ago.'

Felix said his favorite short word of contempt, then, 'Dust yonder.'

'Yeah. The mourners.'

Six riders emerged to view. They dismounted and tied up at the corral, and one came to the house afoot. He was the cocky young giant, Alto, long striding on his high boot heels, with an important clatter to his Spanish spurs, and the drape of his fancy-design gun leather.

'Well, here's your funeral outfit, Felix,' he said. 'If you ask me, Son ain't worth it.'

'I didn't ask you, boy. You-all rest till me and Tully are ready. After the funeral you're going on a hunt for Canary Lenny. I want him brought out here and dealt with proper.'

'Tully told me.' Then, bluntly, 'Sure it was him? What about Son's hotel gal—?'

103

'We're sure enough,' Tully snapped. 'Canary will do, and we got even a better reason to shut him up for good.'

Alto nodded agreement. In a lower voice, he asked, 'How's Prez doin'?'

Felix replied harshly, 'About like you'd expect from the way you done him up that night.'

Alto jerked in resentment. 'Could of been Tully, or any of them—it was pitch dark—'

Tully snapped, 'Shut up, Alto! You're all mouth.'

The two-hundred-pounder looked away from Tully, shut up, and paraded himself back to the corral.

Guiro called from the kitchen and Tully headed down the dogtrot hall. Felix opened the door to Tully's room and began to root for a clean shirt.

*   *   *

Leona left the mule for somebody else to pen and made the long walk down the path through the boulders toward the Mexican adobes. She carried the bundle of laundry and two of Felix's dirty flannel shirts that Guiro had handed her. In a wash tub at the back of the shack, she arranged Prez's bloody sheets and garments, dropped in lye soap, and filled the tub from the water barrel. She looked at Felix's two shirts and slowly began to twist them tightly in her

104

hands. She walked down the weedy path to the outhouse and dropped the two wadded shirts through the hole, seeing them vanish into the dark, filthy pit below. She returned to the house, left the tub of clothing to soak, and went to a small wooden chest in a corner. She dug within it and brought out a slender dagger with a small steel handle. She tried its sharpness with her calloused thumb, then wrapped the blade in a scrap of cloth, sheathlike, and tied it with a torn strip of fabric around her wrinkled thigh above her right knee. Then she stretched on her pallet, careful of the knife, and got her body adjusted for her delayed siesta.

*   *   *

Amanda Forester sat on the front porch of her rambling boarding house, uncomfortably warm in a dark cotton dress, small straw hat, and the sober kind of expression appropriate for wearing to a funeral. Ann Lindsay came around the corner on the clay walk from her room in the south wing. She took a chair beside Amanda and they waited for Amanda's Mexican house boy to bring the buggy. Ann smoothed the skirt of her light linen dress and touched a handkerchief to small beads of perspiration on her upper lip and temples.

The distance between their chairs was only four feet, but a great gulf of space had somehow separated them from the beginning.

105

Amanda, experienced to the ways of Angelo, friendly by nature, had felt not quite at ease with this attractive new-girl-in-town. In her outspoken way, and typical of her earlier years as a cabaret entertainer, Amanda had offered a customary friendliness. But she had never penetrated Ann Lindsay's guarded reserve. It did not matter to Amanda, except as a matter of small curiosity. She had too many other things to concern her than to speculate about the private thoughts of a lady boarder.

Yet the shabby hypocrisy of the day's situation seemed to be tangibly obvious above the small strain which curiously divided them. It was like Amanda to be moved to put it in frank words.

'I've put on several kinds of acts on a lot of stages in my time, but this is the first time I've done such a crude burlesque. Rock-bottom in acting, I'd call it. For Son Hebron. No offense meant, Ann, if you're honestly as grieved as you look.'

Ann hesitated before replying. 'That's not a very nice thing to say. He was my—we had been going together—he was alive last night, with me, and then—and now he is dead.'

'All right. I agree. I didn't mean to prick a tender spot. To me he was just another Hebron, and I had a few years in that wolf pack. I guess I lost all my sense of direction about romance. If you really cared for him, then I'm sorry.' She turned a level glance.

'Pardon my bluntness, but I simply can't understand how you would fall for him.'

The look Ann returned to her was just as direct. 'You fell for one of them yourself, once. Was Son so much worse than Tully?'

'That's a fair answer, honey, and I asked for it. All I can say is that I was younger and ambitious when I met Tully, and to me, at the time, the Hebrons were a big name.' She added softly, 'It's a woman's natural state, being married is, especially if you were a kid making the dance-hall circuit. The road ahead can look awfully long and empty when you look down it all by yourself. Maybe we reach a point when we're not so choosy.'

Ann said quietly, 'I know.' Then, in a tone of husky sincerity, 'You're still young, Amanda, and attractive—there's time enough left.'

'Time goes fast, out here.' Amanda stared into the distance. 'Not long ago I thought I was about to find the one, just the one for that long empty road, and I would have been happy to have had him to walk it with. But something happened . . .'

Ann asked politely, 'You lost him?'

'Uh-huh.' Amanda's voice caught. 'Something like you lost Son. Bullets in the back—but somewhere in Bitter Creek canyon instead of Hooligan's Corral.'

Ann touched the handkerchief to her temples. 'I'm sorry. May I ask you who he was and what happened?'

'Oh—A man who came here. I'll spare you the unpleasant details. And speaking of a new man, your Mr. Victor Scott will be taking his evening meals with us. Didn't *he* waltz right into a peck of trouble? I'm so glad Arch Moon and Felix and Tully turned him loose.' She held a steady appraisal on Ann. 'Made a bad night for you, too. Your first date here with somebody beside Son—'

'It doesn't matter,' Ann said a bit sharply. 'Amanda, you're the nearest substitute to a woman in the Hebron family, I mean having been married to Tully—what would you think about driving out to their place, afterward? I've never been there. Just for a sympathy visit, after the funeral? I imagine Felix would appreciate it.'

Amanda said, 'Good gosh!' Then, smiling, 'Just the idea of old Felix being sad and needing sympathy jolted me for a second. But I don't know. I guess it would be a Christian thing to do, anywhere else, and anybody but that clan.'

'It isn't a long ride,' Ann persisted, 'and we could go together, just as a friendly act, out of respect to Son—'

Amanda shrugged. 'That outfit doesn't much take to visitors. But in a case like this— Yes, at least I *could* cook a decent supper for Felix and Tully. You'll find the house a hogpen.'

'Well, we might do a little cleaning up for

them.'

'All right. My cook can take care of the supper here. Doing that for Felix probably won't be any worse than what we're about to go through with for Son. Here comes the buggy.' As they walked down the steps, Amanda said, 'In all the excitement, you never told me how you made out with Vic Scott. Not so well, I take it, seeing that you ditched him at the dance.'

'He was nice,' Ann said lightly. 'But we really didn't get acquainted. Son came, you know, and he and I went out and talked about—about our plans. And *you* rather took over Mr. Scott, you know. Anyhow, Son had been drinking. I got him to bring me home, and that's the last I saw of Son *or* Vic Scott.'

At the buggy, Amanda impulsively touched Ann's arm. 'You poor girl. Like I said, we find our men and then we lose them.'

'Yes. You know, don't you?' Ann was giving her a studying look. 'First there was Tully, then—who was the other one?'

'His name,' Amanda said, her thoughts seeming far away, 'was Drew Cooper. Not that it matters now. Somehow, even in the beginning I had the queer feeling that it wasn't going to turn out right for me . . . But we live in hope. Now I wonder,' she added impulsively, slapping the lines to speed up the horse, 'if Vic Scott is already spoken for by some beautiful somebody back in Fort Worth?'

'I think so. Only she lives in Austin . . . What

was Drew Cooper like, Amanda?'

Amanda did not answer, and Ann prompted, 'Did you ever learn who did it—the bullets—?'

'Sorry I brought it up,' Amanda said shortly. 'Well, square your shoulders, honey. You'll be undressed right in the graveyard by the eyes of the toughest collection of range hands ever assembled, with Felix's gun practically in their backs, making them come pay last respects to a Hebron.'

'We'll drive right to the ranch afterward,' Ann reminded. 'If we can, let's get there ahead of the others and straighten the house and cook a good meal for them—'

Amanda turned for a kindly look at the slightly pale face beside her. 'You mean well, Ann. I think your heart's in the right place. Even if it is a little difficult to understand you.'

Ann flashed a quick, responding smile. 'Perhaps some day we'll understand each other better, Amanda. I like you.'

'Well!' Amanda breathed with pretended astonishment and flicked the buggy whip. 'This day is turning out better than I ever expected!'

'Yes. Always darkest . . .'

CHAPTER TEN

Riding north from Angelo, Vic Scott followed the wagon tracks which wound through rough country, conscious that at last he was on

Hebron range where few outsiders ever came, and remembering that Drew Cooper had ridden in never to return.

The drink and the talk with Doc Flayhorn had produced no inkling of the location of the Hebrons' sick mare. He had gained nothing but the conclusion that the veterinarian was trouble-laden, close-mouthed and suspicious.

The gray rat of worry that gnawed deepest was how to classify Ann Lindsay.

There was no question about Son's attempt to rape her, and Vic was ready to assume that her grief that morning before Felix and Judge Ed was pretended. But that did not explain her romantic interest in Son in the first place. Nor why she had dated Vic so quickly, had carried a gun, and had been so fully accepted by the Hebrons as an almost-member of the family.

He shifted uneasily in the saddle, keeping a close watch over the country ahead. Considering the way Captain Kincaid was lone-wolfing his part of the mission, he felt that the things needing to be done had dangerously bunched up. He urgently needed a private talk with Ann Lindsay, and there was Amanda Forester to be cultivated, and Doc Flayhorn who should be under surveillance, and Canary Lenny with his secret was in danger of a Hebron lynching as Son's killer. And there was his present venture on Hebron range, the need to play it exactly right, if he was going to scout for a clue to Prez and get out again with a whole skin.

He came to a fork where one set of tracks angled northwest, the other northeast; he had been told to take the right fork to the Bitter Creek graze. The west road circled above a red limestone cut and disappeared through the mesquites toward Felix's headquarters.

Prez, where have they got you, big boy?

In another twenty minutes, at the top of a rise, Vic noticed a far-off dust trace on the other road. Shielding his horse in the trees, he watched until he made out the dots of riders. That would be Felix and his hands, bound for town and Son's funeral. He waited until they had vanished from sight, and considered his chances on scouting the headquarters in their absence. It was an opportunity not likely to come again, he thought; to anyone encountered there he could claim that he had merely taken the wrong trail.

He had reached the decision that he would ride directly across the roughs and find the Hebron headquarters when his eye caught the faint movement blended against a low cliffside in the distance. The rider came toward him and Vic had the feeling the man had been sitting there for some minutes, watching.

As the distance closed, he recognized the half-breed, Chock, who carried a rifle loosely under his right arm.

'Been waitin' for you, Mr. Scott.'

'Well, I'm here, Chock.'

'Yeah. Just keep goin' down the trail you're on. I got a shack a ways ahead. Tully says you're to wait there.'

*　　　*　　　*

Vic had tried all the conversational gambits that he thought might take at least a pawn of information from a range rider in a lonely line camp. The most he had produced in a half hour in the shack was a few grunts from the locked-in Comanche mind. Chock was interested in nothing but sprawling on one of the two bunks, giving his feet a rest. You could spend a lifetime with Chock between siesta and sunset, Vic thought.

He stood up from the bare table and carried the tin coffeepot back to the stove where Chock had boiled for them a stout black cup apiece.

'Coffee's all right but whisky is better,' Vic said, beginning a new try. 'I've got a bottle in my saddlebag. I see you have a deck of cards. Tully is not going to get back in time to show me any cattle before dark, anyhow. So why don't we be sociable?'

For the first time, the impassiveness cracked on the dark Comanche features. Chock was interested. He came off the bunk and began pulling on his boots.

'In that I am an expert, *señor*!'

Vic nodded. 'I'll get the bottle.' He turned

113

for the door. Now that the coffeepot's mighty smell had subsided, another odor caught his nostrils. Very faint, but near at hand; it touched his memory and made him think of Doc Flayhorn.

Chock said, 'You stay. I go. Need to take look.'

Chock picked up the rifle and departed. Vic moved across to the second bunk as soon as Chock's footsteps faded. He bent and sniffed, and turned back two blankets to expose a knotty mattress. He caught the old medicine smell and saw the stain in the fabric. A dark smear, that he believed was Prez Duvall's blood. He tried to respread the blankets as they had been, then went to the closet in the corner. As he passed the open door, he saw Chock in the distance, reaching into Vic's saddlebag and lifting the bottle.

The closet was crowded with sweat-smelly contents. Burrowing into it, Vic dug to the bottom. His hand touched cold iron, and he pulled up a short length of chain. He quickly examined it in the dim light. The chain had been roughly cut; it was stained with a dark dried substance. Hurriedly, he crammed the chain back to its place and heaped the jumble on top of it. *So they brought you here first, Prez, then they moved you.*

As he turned from the closet door, he was thinking that Chock or no Chock, he had to visit Felix's headquarters; and now, while the

114

best chance existed. The afternoon already was racing toward dusk.

Chock stood at the doorway, Indian silent. He carried the rifle and a bottle and his dark protruding eyes were fixed on the closet door.

Vic muttered, 'Where'n hell do you keep your glasses?'

'Up there.' Chock motioned to the shelf beyond the stove. 'Plain sight.'

'All right. Give me the bottle and shuffle the cards. I'll get glasses and water.'

Chock released the bottle, put down his rifle, and went to the table. Vic turned his back, working at the kitchen counter. He poured two thick tumblers three-fourths full of whisky. He heard Chock pull out a chair and start working the cards with gusto. In his right fingers Vic clutched Doc Flayhorn's sleeping pills. He dropped them into one of the glasses of whisky, hoping that they dissolved fast. He delayed until Chock called jovially, then carried the glasses, put the loaded one at Chock's elbow, and carried his own around the table.

Chock pulled out a fold of currency. 'Let's see your money, Scott.'

Vic produced greenbacks. Chock grinned. 'Ho, *damn*—you kiss 'er *adios*!'

'Expert, eh?'

'Whisky, poker—Chock like! Very much damn fun now, eh?' He shuffled with concentration, then put down the deck and took up his whisky. He made a gesture of salute

115

and downed half the whisky without pausing for breath.

'*Wheeeee!* Good damn fire, huh?' Chock smacked the table with his fist. 'I deal. I make the rules—'

Vic thoughtfully took a small swig and watched the swarthy, excited face across the table. *Drink it all, friend—I love a drunk Comanche.*

Chock gleefully won the first hand and raked in the pot and took another gulp from his glass. He turned happier by the minute, then boisterous, then sleepy, and three hands later he had drained the rest of his glass and had decided to burrow his head into his arms folded across the table. The Hebron watchdog snored.

Vic took his hat and jacket from the wall, walked to his horse, saddled, and rode down into the arroyo. He came up a rock-lined trail on the far side and once again rode through the mesquites.

An hour of slow progress brought him to a brushy ravine he took to be Flint Creek and his first look at the spread of the Hebron buildings beyond. He studied the hazy outlines of the big house, the adjacent corrals and shacks.

When he came out of the trees and rode into the open, the sun had gone but daylight lingered. His course brought him in behind three small 'dobes. He could see no movement anywhere, save a flock of chickens in one of the Mexican yards and a few garments flapping on

116

a clothesline behind the nearer shack.

His horse flung its head and waltzed sideways, drawing Vic's attention again to the clothesline which had created the animal's nervousness. He dismounted and walked over, first touching the hanging pair of pants, still damp. His stomach suddenly tightened. He saw the bloodstain, not quite washed out. The other garments and the bed sheets showed the stains, too. He felt eyes on his back, and walked away, searching from under his hat brim for signs of life and seeing none.

He walked quietly to the front of the shack and to its shadowed, open door. He pulled the edge of his canvas brush jacket from over the butt of his Colt as he stepped into the dim front room. He waited for his vision to adjust, and then, suddenly, his hair crawled like a nest of beetles as he heard the faint rustle. It came out of a connecting doorway and he whirled to meet a cat-fast charge of bare feet, fast breath, and glistening teeth. The crouching woman raised her arm and held the blade ready.

Whether she would have struck with it he had no time to decide. He leaped and caught her arm, twisted her off balance, and the dagger fell to the floor. She hovered against the wall, looking up at him through straggling hair, rubbing the pain in her wrist.

He made her out as a frightened old Mexican woman and forced calmness into his tone. 'Why you do this, *señora*? A knife for an innocent friend of the Hebrons?'

She gritted in Spanish, 'Why you come here?'

'You should answer me first. What is your name?'

'Leona. You do not belong here, in my house, looking for what I do not know. They have told you wrong—I am an old woman, I do not sell myself—go hunt the young ones.'

'It is not that. I have just ridden in and I called out but no one answered. I am new here—I wished to inquire for Señor Forester who expects me.'

'Then why you not go to the big house? But they are not back from the funeral.' She seemed to be getting over her fright and anger. He stooped, retrieved the dagger, and extended it to her. Then he took off his hat.

'A thousand pardons, *señora*. It was not my intention to frighten a kind lady. As I said, I only wished to inquire—'

'You inquire first at my clothesline? What you see?'

'I have been long on the road and I expect to be the business guest of the Hebrons. Your clothesline reminded me that my bags are stuffed with dirty clothes. Could I pay you to do a washing for me?'

She thought it over and finally said, 'For a little money, yes.'

'Thank you. Now would you do me the favor, please, of a drink of water?'

118

She hesitated, then padded away to the kitchen. Quickly, he looked into the adjoining room, then turned and opened another door, seeing only a cubby-hole room with a pallet on the floor. No clues here, except the bloodstained garments on the line. So, it would be the other shacks, then, or the big house. Leona came back with water in a gourd dipper.

The dusk was fast closing down and Leona was little more than a blur, blended into the bare wall.

She murmured, 'I do not like you here.'

'Then I will leave. I hope I do not need to tell Felix about the knife.'

She considered that, then said defensively, 'I thought you a new rider, put up to some trick by the others. I will hope that you do not tell Felix or Tully—'

'I will forget. And *you* will forget that I came. I wish you no harm. Is it agreed?'

'*Sí.* It is forgotten.'

'Then we will go together to the next house. You will help me find a washerwoman and I will pay you the same as I pay her for the work—'

'No. You should go to the big house. You see Guiro—it is there you should wait for Señor Hebron. We do not like strangers.'

He made his retreat, walking into the settling night and around the side yard to his horse. Up the slope lamplight was showing in windows of the big house.

119

He dismounted and tied near the front porch and saw that a hitched buggy stood there. So some of the clan had returned from the funeral. But the hallway yawned dark and empty, and no one came. He stood for a moment in the doorway, listening. Kitchen sounds and voices came faintly from the rear. He took three steps and was standing beside the first closed door on his left. He reached and gently turned the knob. The door opened inward with a small squeak of its hinges. His own breath seemed to be pumping louder than the door noise. He carefully closed the door behind him, keeping his hand over the butt of his Colt.

Only the dark blue blur of evening came from the open window, softening the inside darkness, and he saw that the room contained an unmade bed, chairs, and articles of men's clothing scattered about. He sniffed deeply, but could catch no odor that matched Doc Flayhorn's office smell.

Somewhere down the dogtrot a door opened and closed, footsteps sounded, and Vic froze against the wall beside the door. Light movement sounded outside. The knob turned, the hinges made their small song, and the door swung back a few inches toward him. The unseen hand held it there for a time that seemed like an eternity, as if someone peered inside. Then the door was gently pulled closed. Movement outside trailed off very faintly, as if

120

the person walked on tiptoes. Somewhere another door opened and closed loudly, and Vic tensely slipped to the hallway. He paused, looking undecidedly at the doors, four to each side, spaced all the way back to the open night at the other end of the corridor. Sounds beyond the far door on the right indicated the kitchen.

He wanted a look at the other rooms. But any moment someone might walk out of the kitchen, or the Hebrons might ride up at his back, and he would be trapped. Yet, playing only the safe chances was not the way to get results in his business. The final slim gamble sometimes was the one upon which the whole payoff on a case depended. He turned the knob of the next door.

The first inch of space revealed lamplight and produced a low muffled word inside. If Prez Duvall himself had appeared at the door, it could have been no more startling than the feminine voice that asked coldly, 'Yes—who is it?'

He entered, closed the door behind him, and they confronted each other across a littered room that was furnished like an office. Ann Lindsay stared first in disbelief, then with an expression of belated guilt. She stood, like a fawn poised for flight, beside an open desk drawer, clutching a dust cloth in her left hand. As she obviously tried to regain composure, he labored to achieve some for himself.

He removed his hat and unobtrusively

121

flicked his jacket edge over the gun butt. Any way he threw the loop would be the wrong way, so he waited, giving her the first try.

She attempted casualness. 'Well! A prowler in the house.'

He said without smiling, 'Which? You or me?'

'I happen to be cleaning up Felix's office.'

'The chore looks good on you. I like the pink apron. Your gun in the pocket?'

She braced against the desk edge, closing the drawer with the pressure of her thigh. 'I believe this calls for an explanation.'

'I would think so, Ann. I didn't know you were a part of the Hebron household.'

'Explanation by *you*, not me.'

'In time.' He glanced about the room. 'You a guest of the family?'

'You might knock first before you enter a room. It's considered politer than bursting in—'

'Oh, I did that, out front. Nobody came.'

Her dark profile finally had achieved a poker face. 'Did Felix expect you?'

'Of course. We're on a cattle deal.'

'Are you sure you were to come here?' She asked it with penetrating shrewdness. 'They didn't mention it.'

'They were too bowed in grief. Like you.'

'All right, Vic. You're on the edge of trouble. Over what happened last night. I'm trying to protect you.'

'That's kind.' He smiled without humor.

122

'You know who's standing on the edge beside me.'

She shook her head. 'What if I admit that you killed him in cold blood?'

If she was close enough to the Hebrons to have the run of the house, then she had to be classified once and for all as their ally, and dangerous to him. Somehow, this final revelation put a bitter dose in his mouth. He had been trying to deny plain evidence, to himself, when all his wary instincts had repeatedly given warnings.

She said aloofly, 'Well? Did you hear what I asked? What are you thinking, Vic?'

'I was just wondering why you were running from him last night. Who's next on your marriage schedule? Tully, maybe?'

His mocking tone sent color to her cheeks but she kept her voice controlled. 'We're not having a very intelligent conversation. You're being personal and—offensive. Suppose you stick to your crooked cattle deals and let me have my private life. Is that asking too much?'

'It would have been, last night,' he said dryly. 'The way you came out of the brush with your lover in pursuit. Should I have left your private life to itself then, and just walked off?'

A mist came up and clouded her eyes. 'No!' she whispered imploringly. 'Don't hurt me with that, Vic! We must—'

She stopped. He plunged, then, for the vital trade essential to his own security. 'Then we

123

both owe each other something. We stick to the first story, and otherwise keep our mouths shut. I want to make sure you understand that.'

Her eyes showed the hurt. Down deep, he thought, she was frightened. 'You don't have to keep saying it. We have agreed.'

He took a few steps toward her. 'There's just one thing—' He paused, not knowing exactly what he wished to say. Her eyes looked up levelly.

'Yes? What?'

'I guess it's that I'm—disappointed.'

He saw her lips barely tighten. Words began huskily in her throat, but they stayed there, and when she had nothing to say he moved toward the door.

Before he could turn the knob, footsteps hurried along the hallway and the door flew open in his face.

The night was neck-deep in surprises. Even as he was confronted by this one, his mind raced with a way to use it to advantage. He grinned at Amanda Forester's open-mouthed astonishment and asked, 'Am I in time for supper?'

'Vic Scott! For heaven's sake! You startled me.'

'I called from the front and got no answer. So I tried to find my way in—'

'He surprised me, too,' Ann said thinly. 'I'd come in to try to straighten Felix's room a little—'

'Imagine!' Amanda worked thoughtful study from one to the other. Then archly, 'Not a premeditated meeting, I trust!'

'Hardly,' Ann murmured.

'Of course you are in time for supper, Vic! That's exactly what Guiro and I are struggling with in the kitchen. But it *is* a surprise! Where on earth did you drop out of—?'

'The truth is, I was over on Bitter Creek when I sighted your buggy coming this way on the other road.' He smiled significantly at Amanda. 'An evening meal with you seemed more desirable than the same with a half-breed named Chock, who was about to pass out from too much whisky. So I simply followed over.'

She obviously was pleased. She touched his arm intimately and said, 'I'm flattered you would go to the trouble.' Her expression changed. 'Unless you were instructed by Tully or Felix to—not to come here—'

'I don't think it matters. I'm to look at some cattle tomorrow and it's immaterial where we start from.'

'Of course. Well—Ann, shall we take our guest to the front parlor? The rest of them should be here any time.' She kept her hand on his arm as they walked along the passageway and she escorted him into the first room on the right. He saw a large, dusty parlor, lighted by a fancy-shaded lamp, and incongruously containing coyote floor rugs, a spittoon of dented brass, and a shotgun in the corner.

He murmured, 'Nice place, here.'

'It was when I supervised the housekeeping,' Amanda said firmly.

From the door, Ann said with a trace of anxiety, 'I hear horses coming.'

Amanda said, 'Vic, you be right at home. We still have things to do in the kitchen. This is a kind of surprise for them, you know—after the funeral and all. It was Ann's idea—'

He nodded. 'Ann is full of surprises.'

'Isn't she, though! Vic, I'm really flattered that you saw me—us—coming out in the buggy and wanted to come over—I just hope those men are not in a bad humor. They can be, well, rough—But if we don't like it, we three simply can drive back to town!'

Vic took a chair facing the door and said easily, 'I don't think they're going to get rough with me. I carry a mighty big checkbook.'

Amanda laughed and tossed her head approvingly. She seized Ann by the arm, smiled back at Vic, and the two of them hurried down the hallway.

In a moment he heard the sound of horses outside, then silence.

He stretched out his legs and stuck his thumbs in his belt. His ears caught the faint movement outside, passing toward the rear. He waited, mentally following them.

They came in from both open ends of the dogtrot. Felix was the first to appear in the open parlor doorway. He held a sixgun in his

126

hand, half raised, and froze there to stab a false smile and hard, squinted challenge on his guest.

In the hall near at hand, Tully's voice snapped, 'Who is it, Felix?'

'Stone and Chesman!' Felix said harshly. 'Moved in and took over!'

Tully came in and he, too, had a Colt in his hand. Other men bunched beyond the door behind him. There was no pleasure in Tully's expression. 'You a little hard of hearin', Scott? This look like the Bitter Creek line camp?'

'Your boy Chock over there couldn't hold his whisky,' Vic said shortly. He looked Tully in the eye, grinned, and jerked his head. 'Back in the kitchen—women more attractive than a drunk half-breed. When I got twenty thousand dollars to lay on the line, I'm particular who I eat supper with.'

CHAPTER ELEVEN

The wolf pack, stirred by the signs of intruders, began to lower its hackles.

Vic stayed watchful for the one clue. If it did not show quickly, then Prez was nowhere about the Hebron headquarters.

Tully had gone back to the kitchen, and now he returned, making a laconic explanation to Felix, who tried to get it fixed in his mind. 'You say it's Amanda and Ann? Come out just to cook our supper?'

'On account of the funeral. They wanted to do something.'

Felix opened a cupboard and yanked out a bottle. The situation had to knock again at his brain. Not many town people did tender favors for the Hebron outfit.

'Nice. Right nice of 'em.'

He downed whisky in sounds like a horse at a mossy trough, then stood the bottle handy to his reach.

It would be natural for an innocent visitor to wonder about their gun-bristling entrance. Vic said, 'You sure hit home with all your cannon primed. What were you expecting, just from seeing my horse and the women's buggy out there?'

Felix only grunted, but Tully tried to cover it. 'Canary Lenny's on the dodge. Since he waylaid Son, we've been a little edgy.'

It didn't hold much water, but Vic said, 'I see.'

Felix cocked the scarred corner of his mouth, pushed through the men, and disappeared toward the kitchen. Tully turned to a corner of the room, bent, and placed his hat on the floor. Vic saw that the foreman's coat edge momentarily tightened to reveal the shape of a knife handle with its sheathed blade fastened inside Tully's wide-belted pants. Something to remember. A hidden knife revealed the whole nature of a man, if you expected to have trouble with him.

Two of the waiting riders braced their shoulders lazily in the doorway outside the shaded lamp's circle of light. Tall shadows, long arms, features gaunt and sun-blacked. Others waited in the hall behind them. They didn't come in and they didn't go away. Vic had the sensation of being watched from something unknown back in a cave.

Boot heels rattled across the front porch. The men moved to open a space and the young rider, Alto, came through like a one-man parade. He bared his teeth for an arrogant tally of the stranger and reached for the bottle. 'Uncle Felix must of expected me.' He downed a drink with theatrical flourishes. 'You ought to try this, Cousin,' he said to Tully. 'What a mourner needs to brace him after a buryin'.' Tully shoved him back with a cold glance. Alto bared his teeth again at the rebuff and draped a thick leg over the table corner. 'You know who's in the kitchen? Bet they're both in heat and not from the wood stove.'

Tully said in a mumble, 'Yeah, we know.'

'Never thought Amanda could be dragged out here except on a rope.' Alto put on a clownish grin for the men in the door and hall. 'Wonder who's gonna comfort Son's lady-love from the hotel, now that he ain't available on account of a mouthful of clods?' With exaggerated brightness he added, 'Me, maybe?'

Tully seemed to remember the waiting

riders. 'Well, you boys petrified? Get those horses to the corral and tend to 'em.'

One said, 'We was waitin' for somebody to tell us something. Way you and Felix come in boilin'—'

'It's all right. Get on with the mounts and hurry it. The women will have supper ready time you get back.'

Alto evidently had the run of the house and was not included in Tully's orders. He remained when the others had left, and proffered the bottle to Vic. 'You man enough to try Felix's rotgut?'

Vic was prepared to play the visitor who was important enough in his own right, a man with business on his mind, and Stone & Chesman money behind him. He said pointedly, 'I'll pass, sonny. Maybe later with Felix.'

Alto, nettled at being tabbed as an underling, swaggered about the room, twirling his plaited watch leather with his forefinger and making his Spanish spurs rattle. Vic had kept his hearing strained for the sounds he sought in the house. Unless he had missed something, none of them had made an exploration. None had shown an urgency to learn what Vic or the women might have seen, either in the house or elsewhere on the premises.

He now accepted the prime question as having been answered. Prez Duvall was not here.

In one way, it settled something; in another,

it was not so good. It threw the quest back to the whole wide country again. The Mexican woman, Leona, had brought Prez's bloodstained clothes from somewhere else. How far, and from what direction? The best bet, he thought, was to keep Doc Flayhorn under surveillance until he led to the answer. He caught himself wishing Captain Kincaid were handy for a consultation.

Tully and Alto went to the porch together and Vic could hear the mumble of their talk. He caught the name, 'Chock,' and surmised that Tully wanted an investigation of what had happened at the Bitter Creek shack. Tully came back to the parlor and Alto continued toward the back of the house, saying, 'All right, Tully, first thing in the morning.'

To Vic, Tully said, 'I doubt if Felix wants to talk business with you tonight. He's got something else on his mind. Canary Lenny.'

'Any trace of him?'

'We got plenty of men on his trail. Ought to know by morning.'

'You think he will confess, if you find him?'

'Before we get through with him he'll talk his guts out.'

The original job wasn't thorny enough; now he had to save Canary Lenny from a lynching for Texas Ranger Vic Scott's killing of a would-be rapist. Blandly, Vic said, 'We can put off looking at the cattle to a better time. Maybe I should just get back to town and see Felix when he's ready. Guess I shouldn't have butted in

131

tonight.'

Tully made a prolonged study of him, working his cigar steadily. 'You're kinda gaited that way. Showin' up at a bad time.'

He let it hang and Vic took it that Tully was still thinking of the saloon scene, the dance, and Son's death, as well as Vic's presence tonight in headquarters. They would be enough for Tully to start knitting a picture.

'No time's bad for me if I can swing a good cattle deal. The way I work, an owner either wants to trade or he doesn't. There's always another herd over the next hill.'

'Uh-huh.' Tully was finished with his study. 'The girls say you spotted them driving out and followed them over.'

Since he could not be sure how Amanda and Ann had told it, Vic waited, trying to see ahead to any possible trap.

Bluntly, Tully asked, 'Where from did you spot 'em?'

'Why, I took a ride around, thinking I might locate the herd. After Chock waded into the whisky over his head.'

He carried the explanation no further, leaving Tully to fill in the possibility that he had ridden at random and had sighted the buggy on the Flint Creek road.

Tully jumped to another subject. 'When you buy a herd, how do you pay off? I mean, cash or draft?'

'I pay off with a Stone and Chesman draft on

our Fort Worth bank. I reckon you know it's good as gold anywhere in Texas.'

'What's the name of the bank?'

'Stockman's National of Fort Worth.'

'The telegraph's working into Angelo, even if the railroad ain't built in yet. Felix would want the bank here to confirm the payoff by telegram.'

'That's natural. He would have his money in two hours.' Mentally, he pictured the consternation at Stone & Chesman in event of such a crisis. They were going a long way to co-operate with the Adjutant General's office as a cover for Vic, but that strait-laced old firm would never squander twenty thousand dollars on a case like this or any other.

Felix entered in time to catch some of the talk and Tully waited. Felix thoughtfully took up the bottle and the subject together. He said, 'Sounds all right, on the face of it. Now, where would you want delivery?'

'At the nearest railroad. That's customary. That would be Sweetwater.'

'Hell, that's eighty-five miles,' Felix protested. 'Damned long drive. I might make a little concession if the buyer took delivery in this county and figured out his own way to get 'em to shipping pens.'

The ice of the trade was being broken. Vic matched the inquiring squint. 'What kind of a concession, maybe?'

'Well, say a dollar a head rebate. For the

133

buyer's trouble.'

Vic said thoughtfully, 'That might be arranged. I don't work for my health.'

'It wouldn't have to show on your records, Scott. Smart man like you would know how to fix the bill of sale.'

'Yes. Sounds fair enough. That's the way I'd want to handle it.'

'Then you could draw your own expenses for moving the stuff to Sweetwater. You commission buyers ought to know the way of doing a thing.'

'I know. You send word when you're ready to show the stuff. Let me get it straight, now—' Ann and Amanda had come to the doorway, but he finished. 'A dollar a round rebate on a thousand head. Price to be written up as twenty dollars. Delivery to me on your own range and I provide the riders to move 'em to Sweetwater. That right?'

'Yeah. Soon as the bank telegraphs Fort Worth.'

Vic thought, *Goddam the newfangled telegraph line.* Those wires could stretch his neck.

'The stuff in good trail shape? All branded?'

Felix lowered one eyelid. 'Why everything's just legal as hell, Scott.' He took up the bottle and grinned at the two women. 'We're talkin' big money, girls. Your old Uncle Felix and Mr. Scott're on a fancy deal. He's a slick 'un.'

Ann Lindsay's fingers worked with the edge

134

of her cook apron. She gave one cool look at the slick 'un who was so openly taking a bribe, then ignored him. Alto's meaty frame loomed from the hall and he crowded beside Ann. 'Hey, let's me an' you go down to the bunkhouse and fetch the boys for supper. Be a nice little walk to build up a appertite.'

A shadow went over her face and she moved a few inches away from him. 'I'd better stay and help Amanda.'

'Aw, come on with me—' Alto caught her arm and drew her toward the door.

'No, Alto—' His fingers tightened with pleasure. She said, 'You're hurting my arm.'

Amanda said firmly, 'Not if she doesn't want to, Alto. Tully, will you please tell that fancy fool to mind his manners. Anyone who goes off in the dark with him will lose their appetite.'

Ann's first small resistance had turned, by now, into a full seesaw struggle with Alto. Vic looked hard at Tully, then at Felix. They were unmoved by the incident. Instead, Tully had been fired by a sudden resentment at his former wife. Amanda's face was flushed and her hair was slightly disarranged, but she looked even prettier and somehow enticing in the yellow and gray lamp shadows.

Tully twisted the cigar out of his mouth. 'Don't you come out here tryin' to give orders to ever'body. Just stick to your cookin'—'

Ann was saying, 'No, Alto—!' and trying to keep her voice calm.

'Aw, go on with the boy!' said Felix with a noticeably thickening tongue. He waved the bottle. 'Amanda was always one to spoil fun. You go on, Ann—he ain't gonna bite. If he does, you bite him *back*!' Felix laughed a thin bray and lifted the bottle.

Alto pulled Ann into the darker hallway by main strength. Her last glance back was divided between Vic, sitting with every muscle taut as iron clamps, and Amanda whose mouth had drawn into a tight wire. Ann's expression was one of mixed helplessness and appeal. Vic moved with the goading that propelled him and crossed the room in savage anger. He heard Amanda's murmured warning as he passed her, then he was on the porch and alongside Alto.

'I'll take the walk with you. Need to stretch my legs.'

Alto's arm dropped from Ann's waist. She moved away, pushing her hands against him.

Alto stopped. 'Well, the city sonofabitch come to life. Just step out here in the yard with me, *hombre*—'

'Wait, Vic!' Ann cried urgently. 'It's all right. I'd really like to walk down to the bunkhouse with Alto—'

'Hear that, Fort Worth? You just crawl back inside before I dust the yard with you.'

They moved on in the cool starlight toward the distant bunkhouse. Shaking a little from an assault of mixed emotions, Vic returned to the room where three sets of eyes fastened on him.

Then Amanda whirled to Felix. 'You and your pack of hyenas!'

Felix snorted his one-word expression of contempt. 'Tully, she's still the trouble maker.'

'Uh-huh.'

Her dark eyes burned, her cheeks reddened. 'I had to pull a knife on Alto once to hold off the kind of attention he always has in mind. Only one decent man ever came on this range in all that time—and you know what happened to *him*!'

Vic watched the touched-off hostilities, conscious of old resentments being exposed.

Felix's droopy grin had gone. 'Trouble maker she is!' he growled accusingly at Tully as if his foreman was to blame.

'She knows when to keep her mouth shut.'

'She's a woman and a woman always gabs.'

'You leave it to me, Felix. She knows when she's in good health.'

Amanda's eyelids batted at sudden tears. Her lips trembled from the intensity of her emotions. 'I know about Drew Cooper!'

The name she uttered pushed Tully into three quick strides toward her. Her hands flew up as his fast back-handed slap cracked against her protecting wrists. She reeled off balance. Vic forced himself to stay put.

Tully stood over her. Amanda straightened and retreated. She forced a weak smile. 'You can see why I finally departed from these fine people, Mr. Scott.'

137

'Just go get supper on!' Tully gritted. 'It's what you came out here for, wasn't it? Or was it?' He shot a hard glance at Vic Scott. Vic took it that a galling jealousy still smoldered in Tully.

She left the room. Felix worked a beady squint on Vic. 'You know anything about what she was spoutin' off?'

He shook his head. 'No. The commotion was a little too thick for me to follow.'

'She never got bridle broke,' Felix mumbled. 'Tully, you got to handle her.'

Vic reached for his hat. 'This doesn't seem like a time to talk business. I'll ride back to town, so as not to intrude on the family supper. Suppose we get together in the next day or two and look at your cattle?'

Felix considered, drew a nod of agreement from Tully, and replied, 'All right. I'll send word when I'm ready.'

They offered no words of good-by and Vic went alone to the porch, and on to his horse at the tie rail. Laughter and voices floated up from the lighted door of the bunkhouse. Men emerged there, Alto and Ann among them. They came up in a straggling group with Alto in the lead, his arm about Ann, half lifting her.

When they had almost reached the house the group slowed, halted and went quiet. Vic also caught the sound of oncoming hoof beats. The rider came out of the darkness.

Someone said, 'It's Bo Hammer. What's the

138

news, Bo?'

The rider swung down. Felix and Tully had come to the porch. Felix called, 'Any luck, Bo?'

'We got him,' the rider reported. 'We hauled in Canary.'

Ann Lindsay quickly turned her head toward Vic who stood beside his horse at one side of the group.

'Where'd they grab him, Bo?'

'Holed up in a Mexican shack on the edge of town. We took all them houses apart.' He added, 'Arch Moon said to bring word to you.'

'That's good. Damn good. Now, tomorrow, I got a few things to see about. We'll just let Mr Lenny cool his tail in the calaboose a while and worry over what's gonna happen to him. Then, when I'm ready, we'll take him off Arch's hands and give him a little trial out here. For murderin' my nephew. Now, you boys come in and eat supper. The girls have been real nice, and you bastards scrape your boots and mind your manners at the table.' He turned and stalked ahead down the dogtrot.

They paraded on to the porch and none bothered to give Vic further notice. He swung into the saddle and pulled the horse toward the road south. Throwing a look back over his shoulder, he saw Ann trying to peer after him before Alto and the others crowded her out of his vision.

He gave his attention to the wagon trace ahead. The tracks lay dim in the starlight, the dwarf mesquites all about pale with ghostly weaving in the night breeze. As he rode his mind raced with the tangled questions of Ann Lindsay and Canary Lenny, the big double problems, and finally all issues gave way to the grim truth standing out—it was his own immediate responsibility to somehow save Canary Lenny.

He passed the fork of the Bitter Creek route without being challenged there, though the actions of the horse told him his passing was observed by some hidden lookout. He topped the last crest above the town in mid-evening and followed the road into the first fringes of the Mexican adobes, crowded in ugliness like a mass of untended chicken coops. Lights gleamed at some of the windows along the main street. The distant courthouse and jail were dark, and so was the second floor of the wagon yard building.

He rode on to the rent stable, turned in the horse, and paid the old man who was eager to speak the news.

'They got 'im! They caught Canary Lenny, the one that killed Son Hebron. He's down yonder at the jail this minute.'

It was the talk everywhere. Vic heard it again from the waitress when he ate supper, and from the night clerk in the Lehman House. In room 24 he lighted the lamp, left the window shade partly up, and went through the motions of taking off his gunbelt, jacket and shirt. He took

140

off one boot and then hobbled across to the window. Naked to the waist, he stood there a moment, prolonging a duel with the jumpy window shade until it was secured, an inch from the bottom. He waited on the far side of the room for five minutes, then blew out the lamp. He went back and raised the shade half to the top at the open window. The wagon yard windows in the distance were still dark.

He maintained the vigil until a few minutes past midnight, and no lights, no socks hanging to dry, appeared at Kincaid's window. His lids became too heavy to trust himself to remain awake longer. He was ready to abandon any prospect of seeing Kincaid tonight. The worry gnawed that perhaps Kincaid was over there in bed, after all, whisky-dead to the world. In either case, Vic could think of nothing they could do for Canary Lenny tonight.

He was about to yield to the inviting bed when the small sound in the hallway brought him back to tense wakefulness. The movement was at his door. The knock came as two cautious raps, as if made with a small and timid fist.

CHAPTER TWELVE

The whispered name barely came through the door to his hearing.

'Ann Lindsay!'

He opened the door, hurried her inside, looked quickly into the deserted corridor. He locked the door again and replaced his revolver in its holster.

'Vic! I had to see you!' Her words were whispered in a flood of anxiety. 'About Canary Lenny! They'll lynch an innocent man!'

He steered her to a chair and sat on the edge of the bed close to her. 'First, how did you come here? Who saw you?'

'Through the back yard and up the outside stairs. I had a key to the gate lock. Nobody saw me—I hope.'

'From where?'

'From my room. As soon as I thought Amanda was asleep. Vic, *something* has to be done!'

'How did you leave your house?'

'By the side door!' she said impatiently. She clutched the brocaded bag he remembered, and he assumed the little gun was inside it.

'What went on after I left your friends, the Hebrons?'

'Amanda and I left as soon as we could. They intend to do something horrible to Canary Lenny. It's our fault—well, *my* fault. You think I led Son on, and I guess I did. But you don't understand. All I care about now is that we just can't let them kill Canary—'

'I don't intend to let him be lynched any more than you do.'

'You just don't know the Hebrons. Vic, what

142

can be done?'

'What do you suggest?' he asked grimly. 'That I confess? Take Canary's place in jail? Then you could step forward, and explain to the Hebrons and the town that your friend Son was shot because he was about to—'

He left the rest unsaid. In a moment she spoke with calm decision. 'Yes, if it's necessary. Whatever trouble it caused me, or even you, I couldn't sit by and let an innocent man die for something he didn't do.' Both of them were silent for a space, then she asked simply, 'It's just a question of right or wrong, isn't it? Is there any other way to look at it?'

'No. I'm glad to hear you say that, and it's the way I see it. You puzzle me, and have from the first time I saw you. You're right at home in the bosom of the Hebron outfit. Thick with Felix, playing coy with Alto, damn near engaged to Son, even crying on Judge Ed's shoulder and out there cleaning house for that rat pack. Considering all that, then why in the name of heaven can't you protect Canary by concocting some story? You've got influence with your fine tribe of bucks!'

She recoiled at his harshness. 'No, Vic! It isn't like that—'

'I don't know why it should matter with me,' he said more mildly. 'But somehow I'm disappointed.'

'And I'm disappointed in you!'

'In what way?'

143

'I'm just sorry, I guess, that you are a dishonest cattle buyer, that you would deal with the Hebrons when no decent buyer would, and cheat your company—'

'All right. I make a little money on the side in a cattle deal. I justify that because I work hard, and my company will make plenty of profit, anyhow. But you—you slip off to Hooligan's Corral with Son Hebron when you're old enough and have been around him long enough to know he's just going to have one idea on his mind when he gets you down there—then you go out to that outlaws' nest to *cook supper*, for God's sake, after the funeral! Leave it that we're both disappointed. Let's drop that and get back to Canary.' As he had talked, she had withdrawn her hand from under his, and replaced it over his fingers, and by the time he had finished she had tightened her grip as if to cut off what he said.

Vic went on, 'If by some lucky means we could help Canary break jail tomorrow night, before the Hebrons took over, where could he be hidden until we slipped him out of the country? Any idea?'

'I don't know. Couldn't he just strike out?'

'They'd run him down if he took to open country. He'd have to hole up first, until we found a way to smuggle him out. It would have to be some place they would never think of searching.'

She thought in concentration, then

144

whispered, 'I know! Amanda's!'

'What?'

'In a room at Amanda's. They'd never think of looking there.'

'You would trust her to hide him?'

'Yes, I think so.' Then, with more conviction, 'Yes, I would trust her. Even if—if I had to tell her a secret.'

'That I killed Son, eh?'

'Well, that—and something else.'

He considered that, found it not to his liking, but could think of no better suggestion. 'Well, we haven't got that far yet. It might do. It's all assuming that Canary can be sprung free, which is problem number one, and the biggest.'

'Yes. Do you have any idea at all how it could be done?'

'None at the moment.' In the back of his mind loomed an appeal to Paul & Co., whoever he was. The federals had told the A.G. they didn't want their water muddied, unless the undercover Rangers had their backs to the wall. God knew his back was almost to the wall now, with Canary due for a lynching, Prez Duvall's whereabouts still unknown, and Captain Kincaid trying to drown an old man's bitterness in whisky.

But the enormity of the Canary Lenny problem towered over everything else. Along with that, Vic pondered an inclination to risk using this moment of advantage, the new intimacy of conspiracy, between himself and this mysterious, attractive woman, to press for more. He mentally tallied back, seeing how his evaluation of her had played from one side to another like a tricky compass needle, from trust to distrust.

He kept his mouth close to her ear so he could murmur quietly, and carefully framed his question. Even her evasion could be revealing if he listened carefully, using his small experience in courtroom trials. His concentration would be on how she responded, what small hesitation or awkward lie to listen for, what the surprise of it might shock out of a woman already agitated.

'Ann—there's a long chance we might help Canary if we could invent a story. Say, a story to make the Hebrons think Prez Duvall had trailed Son down and killed him for some reason. That would depend, of course, on Prez being able to get up and around, so he could have slipped out and followed Son to Hooligan's Corral. I wonder if Prez is anywhere near, and able to do that?'

He watched her features in the semidarkness. He made all his senses strain to a sensitive edge to catch her first reaction before she put on control.

He registered the sequence. First, there was her face tilting for a blank look at him; next, a pause for her thoughts to work, and quickly after that, the decisive shake of her head. All honest enough. Next he waited for her voice

146

tone, though a tone could be controlled by a clever liar after a few seconds to get it ready.

'I don't know,' she murmured doubtfully. 'Prez might have had a reason. But from what little I've heard, he's wounded too badly to be walking around. I don't have the slightest idea where he's hiding.'

The hell of it is, everything she's ever said to me rings with honesty.

'You mean Son never confided in you?'

'Not to that extent, he didn't.'

'Well, we've got to go at it some other way. Maybe it wasn't a very good idea. I'm just groping for a way to help Canary.'

She said forlornly, 'I don't know how we're going to do it, just the two of us, against all of *them*. But there's no one but us who knows that Canary is innocent, or would try to do anything for him—'

For one sudden moment of fleeting wonder he played with a wild and improbable chance. 'Ann,' he asked with deliberation, 'do you know of any cattle buyer here connected with Paul and Co.?'

'No, Vic. Why?'

'Not important. Just forget I asked you ... Hadn't you better go, now? Longer you're here, more the risk.'

She stood almost against him. 'Please, Vic, tomorrow night. We'll have to help Canary—'

He placed his arm about her, holding her and she yielded for a minute, as if needing

147

strength for something too heavy for her shoulders. He felt the yielding and knew that he liked holding her close. Gently, she pulled away, and he guided her into the hallway and watched her fade like a shadow to the end of the corridor. He kept his attention alert to all the intervening doors.

Then he followed silently down the hall. Her movement was barely visible from the rear door as she disappeared through the gate which she had to leave slightly ajar because she could not turn the key in the lock when it was in Vic's pocket. During the brief embrace, he had merely slipped two fingers down into her dress pocket and removed the key to his own.

He descended the wooden steps, silently cursing every squeak of the boards. He kept to the shadows and edged along the fence with his alertness tuned to the windows in the back of the hotel. Then he was through the gate and in the alley, and spotted her distant, hurrying form as she neared the side street. He let her walk a block ahead as he moved, pressing close to the building fronts. Once she paused for a backward look, then hurried on. He trailed in the trees along a road between scattered houses. He watched from concealment as she reached Amanda's darkened house and saw her enter the side door. Getting to the house, and to her window, involved risks, but he chanced it. With his ear pressed to her shaded window, he listened for any give-away voices

148

and heard none. She made no light, and finally he heard the faint sound of bed springs giving to her body.

He began his return, as noiselessly and as cautiously as he had come, and mentally wrote another small mark in her favor. No one had seen her; more important, none had been waiting for her to report.

At the high back wall of the hotel yard he waited and listened, pressed against the boards just outside the gate and uncertain whether he had heard an alien sound. A pen of turkeys in the hotel yard had been stirred up and were making uneasy movements along their roost. In some nearby back yard a calf bleated and a cow bawled. The gate, Vic thought, was opened wider than he had left it.

He edged inside the opening and made a scrutiny of the pitch-dark rear yard and its untidy scattering of crates, poultry pens and trash piles. He froze. All his nerves bristled. Some alien something that looked like a human shape was crouched against the stairs' wood railing with its head slanted upward toward the ascending steps.

He advanced noiselessly and was almost upon the motionless figure when it whirled and discovered him. Vic closed the remaining distance and jabbed hard with his Colt into the shrinking softness.

'Don't move. Keep your voice to a whisper.' He punched the gun muzzle deep into a belly.

149

He strained to make out the man's features. He had the vague feeling this was someone he knew.

'Who are you?'

The angle of the head showed the other man was trying to identify Vic. There was barely enough light from the sky to make possible their simultaneous discovery.

'You're Mr. Scott, ain't you? I was comin' to your room. I'm Canary Lenny.'

'*For God's sake!*'

'I was just tryin' to get up my nerve—'

Taking a firm grasp on Canary's scrawny shoulder, Vic roughly shook him for silence. He looked toward the gate, half expecting a whole army of pursuers. A flood of questions tumbled in his mind. He tugged Canary in a retreat to the alley. It wouldn't take an army of Arch Moon's posse men to ruin him now—just one chance witness to any connection between Canary and him would be his undoing.

He brought his mouth close to Canary's ear. 'One question—you know any hide-out place we can get to *quick?*'

'No. None around here.'

Vic's mind caught at Ann's suggestion. Amanda Forester. Any gamble now was a long one. It was no time to sort and choose.

'Listen to me. Just nod your head if you understand. When I get to the end of the alley, you start. I'll turn left. You follow. Keep in the shadows, just keep me in sight. If anybody

150

jumps you, tear out the best you can and never say my name, understand?'

Canary nodded vigorously.

Vic struck down the alley, his boots seeming to clang his going for all the town to hear. The walk to Amanda's house became a tightrope over a waiting chasm. He guessed the time at past two o'clock. He covered the final stretch of the sandy road and stood weak-legged and sweaty at the porch corner. Canary Lenny dodged forward, an uncertain shadow slipping from the trees. In another moment, Vic was tapping at Ann's window.

He heard the bed springs give, then her low inquiry at the window.

Tersely, he gave instructions, and cut her off with, 'Move fast, now.'

The next wait seemed longest of all as he stood with the fast-breathing Canary. When the front door creaked open, he steered Canary ahead, past the two women, and waited until Amanda led the way along a corridor. Finally, she groped for him and placed a lamp in his hands.

He said, 'See that the windows are covered.'

He placed the lamp on the floor in a far corner, touched a match to the wick, and turned it low. Three strained faces floated across the room in ghostly white. Amanda and Ann stood together, nervously clutching their robes, with flimsy edges of nightgowns showing above their bare feet. Their features, scrubbed of cosmetics for the night, were pale and stark with wonder. Canary, a haggard and unsavory item of debris from out of the dark, licked his dry, fuzzy lips and gave off the odor of jail, alkali dust and old chili peppers, all mixed with the stench of fear sweat.

Ann asked, 'How on earth—?'

'Just a minute.' Vic motioned to Amanda. 'Can anyone in the other rooms hear talking in here?'

'Not if we keep our voices down. One side's the dining room and the other is the front parlor.'

'I want a few minutes with Canary. Will you and Ann wait somewhere? Don't light a lamp.'

The two of them left, moving close together as if for protection, and Vic motioned for Canary to come near.

'Just listen to what I ask you. Give me answers right to the point and keep your voice down . . . How did you get out of jail?'

'Sawed the bars. Crawled through the window.'

'Where'd you get the saw?'

'Somebody poked it through the window.'

'Why did you come to me?'

'Whoever it was, he said to. Through the bars when he dropped in the hacksaw. He said, "Go to Mr. Victor Scott, room 24, Lehman House." I sawed for about two hours. That sheriff and deputy, they don't stay there, just an old man on guard. He was up front asleep.

When I got through I come to the back of the hotel—'

'That was all he said? Just come to me?'

'Yeah. I saw something move up high in the window and went over and it was the saw poking through. When I caught hold of it, somebody outside said to come to you, and that was all—I never saw hide nor hair—'

'You didn't know the voice?'

'No, sir. He just sorta growled it.'

'You know why you were sent to me?'

'No, sir. I didn't have no time to figure.'

'Do you know my job here?'

'Yeah. You're a cattle buyer.'

'After they hauled you in, did Sheriff Moon and Deputy Tabor or any of the Hebron men question you about Son Hebron's death?'

'Not yet. I think they was gonna start on me today. Honest to God, Mr. Scott, wasn't me that killed him.'

'Do you know Prez Duvall?'

'Yeah. I used to work for the Hebron outfit.'

'You know where he might be hiding out?'

He saw Canary hesitate. 'Not exactly.'

'What do you mean, "not exactly"?'

'I might have a idear.'

'Well, what is it?'

'Why would *you* want to know?'

'Listen, damn you—you want me to save your neck or turn you over to Felix and Tully?'

Wretchedly, Canary said, 'Ain't nobody else to help me outta this perdicament, Mr. Scott.

153

I'd almighty appreciate if you'd help me—'

'Then where do you think Prez is holed up?'

Canary was suffering. He rolled the whites of his eyes and said plaintively, 'Can't you hide me somewhere now? I'm all comin' apart, I been that scared. Tomorrow we could talk.'

There was more that Vic felt compelled to drag out of Canary but there was no more time to risk. He summoned Amanda and Ann. 'Are you willing to hide him here?'

Amanda said, 'Yes. Ann has convinced me that he's innocent, and I thought so, anyhow. He can stay in a little storeroom off my bedroom.' Even under strain her somewhat bawdy sense of humor came out, and Vic had to grin when she added, 'Just so long as it isn't in *my* clean bed!'

She took the lamp and led the way, across her own room and to a door which revealed a small storage room equipped with an Army cot. 'He could stay here indefinitely. They'd never think of looking in my house, anyway.'

Vic asked bluntly, 'No one ever comes to your bedroom?'

She arched her brows and exclaimed, 'Why, *Mister* Scott!'

*   *   *

He walked the long tight rope of tension, back through the trees along the sandy road, then in the store shadows, into the alley. Once again he slipped through the gate and locked it behind

154

him. He reached the stairway. The pen of turkeys had quieted.

He took a deep breath of relief when he finally locked the door of room 24. Squinting into the night from the window, he saw only darkness at the wagon yard. He undressed and as he walked across the carpet he idly thought of the ashes of Ellen Johnston's burned letter beneath it. For some reason not clear, he thought that everything between Ellen and him was ashes now, and it had happened somewhere on this assignment; the exact time, place and reason unknown. He got into bed, and the recent presence of Ann Lindsay lingered there in the chair beside it, within reach of his hand. A girl who baffled him, but one who would take personal risks to save a prairie waif like Canary Lenny simply because it was, as she had said, a question of right and wrong.

But at least a great load had been lifted. Canary Lenny was safe, for the moment, from a Hebron lynching. Delivered by an unseen benefactor with a hacksaw out of the night.

He fell asleep, his last conscious thought being a new appreciation for the alertness and ingenuity of Captain Kincaid.

CHAPTER THIRTEEN

Sun fire and the heat of a new day struck the cactus hills and greasewood sinks and at one livid stroke wiped out the brief gray dawn.

Suddenly the town's lumber and adobe walls were splashed with a brassy glitter. This Saturday in Angelo seemed to start faster than usual, crackling alive with hoof beats and harsh voices. The news had hit swiftly, bounding the length of main street, fanning out on the roads and trails.

There had been a jail break. Canary Lenny was at large. The Hebrons were on the warpath.

Vic heard the first fragments of the excitement floating up to his room as he shaved and dressed. There was more of it in the hotel lobby, on the sidewalks, and among the late breakfast patrons at the café. Talk had it that Tully Forester already was leading a house-to-house search of the Mexican settlement, and that Deputy Sam Tabor had taken another posse to scour the range southward toward the border. Both Sheriff Moon and Deputy Tabor had caught a brutal tongue-lashing from the boiling-mad Felix Hebron. Felix and Tully, summoned at once when the break was discovered by the jail guard before daylight, had taken full charge of the search.

The hour was near ten o'clock when Vic emerged from the café and stood on the plank walk, listening to the talk of a small knot of men. All of them turned as new activity was sighted at the courthouse grounds. A delegation filed out of the jail office and mounted. Six of them rode west and Vic recognized the stocky Alto in the lead. The others rode eastward into the mesquites.

'There go some more of Felix's itchy triggers.'

'They're sure to pick up his trail somewhere,' another said. 'When they do it'll be bullets for Canary.'

Returning to the Lehman House, Vic saw that Ann Lindsay had come to work. She and Charlie were busy at the desk where a few idlers had congregated to talk. She glanced up and they exchanged a full and significant look as he crossed the lobby. He climbed the stairs to his room. He raised the shade and saw the socks hanging in the distant window of the wagon yard.

A short time later he went up the outside steps to the wagon yard's second floor. When Captain Kincaid first surveyed Vic his usual sourness seemed tempered with a new respect.

'You got the town boilin',' Kincaid grunted. 'Let's have a quick check-up on this thing. Sit down.'

Whatever doubts he'd had about the crusty veteran, Vic had to admit that Kincaid had smartly delivered him from a bad, almost hopeless complication. So he said with crisp sincerity, 'Captain, you pulled a neat trick, getting that hacksaw to Canary.'

Kincaid, halfway to a chair, froze as if he had discovered a steel trap in his path. He turned a puzzled expression to Vic.

157

'Me?'

Vic felt his tongue go dry. 'The hacksaw you smuggled—'

Kincaid blinked. 'Wasn't me. By damn, I thought *you* did it!'

They held the unsavory revelation between them like a live coal being handed back and forth. The silence stretched, the truth sunk in a little, then for Vic it gouged in all the way, and it changed everything.

'This is bad,' he muttered. 'Whoever did it sent Canary to me. Somebody knows.'

'You're spotted!' Kincaid said harshly. 'Something's leaked. Damn it to hell, you've tipped us, somehow.'

Kincaid took an agitated turn in the cramped space. The smell of whisky lingered in the room despite the fresh air of morning. Vic, shaken with doubts, tried to check back to the point where exposure had come, and could not find it. Yet, a third somebody, unknown, had boldly revealed knowledge of a link between Canary Lenny and the Stone & Chesman cattle buyer, perhaps knew that Vic had killed Son Hebron.

Kincaid demanded, 'Who could have got you tabbed? That girl?'

'I don't know. But not her. Maybe we're just jumping at conclusions as to whoever it was knowing my real job.'

'How else can you dope it?'

'I had sided Canary before a saloon full of

people and had another run-in with Son's friends at the dance. Maybe Canary's man with the hacksaw only gambled that I'd help him. It could be just coincidence—not what it looks like, that it connects with our other business.' He didn't have much conviction in what he was saying and his tone showed it.

'Yeah, and it could be somebody who knows you done in Son!' Kincaid retorted. 'Mighty damn strange, and full of stickers. Any idea who?'

Vic could think of no one. 'Likely some friend of Canary's, willing to go far enough to slip him the saw but not up to staying around to help him get holed up.'

'Let's nail down the fact. Somebody knows Canary beelined to you last night. If one knows, a dozen others could. I ask you, *Sergeant*, how long you think that'll take to get to Felix Hebron?'

'I've already said it's not good, Captain.'

'Not good!' Kincaid snorted with contempt. 'Hell, it could ruin us both. Likely nullifies all the damn effort I put in, workin' half the night on something . . . But fill me in. What've you done with him?'

The answer to that, Vic knew, was going to be the last straw, as far as Kincaid's displeasure was concerned. He worked up to it by describing his day on the Hebron range, Ann Lindsay's visit to his room in the night, the later coming of Canary. Reluctantly getting to the delicate point, because he knew Kincaid would not like it, he told how he had hidden Canary at Amanda Forester's house.

Kincaid chewed on that for a moment as if his mouth was filled with gravel. 'Now two women are mixed up in it. One of them Son's gal and one Tully's ex-wife. Boy, your hide is nailed to the barn. If those two women hold their tongues they'll be the first females in history that done it. A mess, Scott. A complete bog-hole mess all around.'

Vic thought there were a few favorable points to be salvaged and attempted to point them out. 'I've gotten on the Hebron range and off again, with enough to warrant the guess that Prez is not out there. And I've fixed them to smell money. I'm dangling twenty thousand dollars under Felix's nose, he's in bad need of cash, and for the time being at least we're friends. And we've got Canary on ice to tell us anything he knows, soon as I can get to him and start pumping.'

Gazing out the window, Kincaid said almost forlornly, 'I think you've also got Miss Ellen Johnston on your mind and that Austin law practice.'

Vic bridled with resentment. 'That has nothing to do—'

'And the hotel filly, Ann Lindsay. Was talk all she come to your room for last night?'

'That was all.'

'She's hand-in-glove with that bunch.'

'I'm beginning to doubt that, Captain.'

'Then find out! When you go to Amanda's to question Canary, scheme some way to search Ann Lindsay's room. One little clue—that's all we need. There're too damn many unknown quantities in this case.'

Vic's mind worked in a jumble of contradictions. One was the curious realization that despite what Kincaid had said, Ellen Johnston hardly had been in his thoughts in recent days. Another was an admittance of how much he was hoping, for a reason still vague, that Ann Lindsay would emerge from this completely above suspicion as a Hebron ally.

He took his hat and was moving to the door when Kincaid stopped him. 'I got took with a hunch yesterday. Way I work. So I spent most of the night layin' in the brush. Watchin' a house. That one yonder.' He gestured, and Vic joined him at the window.

Judge Ed Hebron's house was a distant dot in the heat vapors, shielded by a stand of poplar trees at the windmill tank. It stood isolated on the far edge of town, flanked by a fenced horse pasture, barn and outhouses, and then mesquite growth disappearing over a ridge to empty country.

Vic asked, 'Did you spot anything?'

'Nothing. But that don't bother me. He blew out the light early and nobody came and nobody went. Somehow, I still like the idea. What'd you think?'

161

'It's possible,' Vic mused aloud. 'Right here in town. Even makes sense, in a way.'

'Yeah. Handy for Doc Flayhorn. Bachelor place, nobody else around, maybe Son was stayin' at nights to help. Last place anybody would expect.'

Scott looked at the gaunt old-timer, picturing him through an uncomfortable night in a mesquite clump, quietly working out a hunch that long experience had told him to follow. The lone-wolf way, but it had always got results.

'Scott, what if I can work up a little whisky drinkin' and poker game with Judge Ed tonight in the Cactus Queen? You up to taking a little look in that house while I occupy him?'

'I'm up to it.'

Kincaid dug into a pocket. 'Here's an extra key to this room, so you can get in if I'm not here. I want to move fast, Scott, from now on. Time comes in a case where every extra day adds to the chance for something to go wrong and your ass shot off. There's the women liable to talk, and there's this hacksaw friend that links you and Canary, and there's Felix ready to call your hand on twenty thousand dollars for his cattle. That's something that worries me, for it ain't gonna hold water forever. I've picked up enough to know Felix needs money bad. Time's comin' when you'll be square up to paying off on this cattle deal and when it does you're caught in a bind. Soon as you stall, Felix

162

is goin' to smell the rottenest mouse he ever sniffed, and he's an expert on that.'

*   *   *

Events within the next hour backed up Kincaid's speculation all the way. Vic, when he returned to the hotel, saw that Ann was watching for him. She motioned him to the desk. Her eyes showed the dark hollows of strain and sleeplessness. 'Felix Hebron sent word that he wants to see you, Mr. Scott.' She spoke formally, because Charlie and others were talking within earshot.

'Where is he, Miss Lindsay?'

'At the jail office. He said he wanted you to come right away.'

He touched his hat to her and returned to the street. When he reached the jail grounds the loungers there were watching a rider who came in at a gallop, and Vic recognized him as Deputy Tabor. The deputy was sweaty and dust powdered. He dismounted and started for the jail.

One of the men called, 'Any trace, Tabor?'

Tabor curtly replied, 'Not yet,' and entered the jail office. Vic followed behind him. Felix had taken charge at the desk. Arch Moon, looking browbeaten and sick, hunched his bulk in the chair opposite. They and the other men in the room sourly glanced at Vic in the doorway before returning their attention to

163

Tabor.

'Nothing south,' Tabor reported. 'I've got my men spread and riding to keep dragging for sign. Anything new from Tully's bunch?'

'Water hauls!' Felix grumbled. He glared at Moon. 'Bunch of numbskulls.'

'Maybe Tully will have something,' Moon said painfully.

'Well, get up and get movin'!' Felix blasted. 'You won't find him sittin' here. All of you—keep at it!'

Moon and Tabor and the others silently trooped out. Felix gave his attention now to Vic who had taken Moon's place across the desk.

'Scott, I reckon you got no idea atall how Canary broke out. So I won't ask you.'

But it was a question, loaded with Felix's suspicion.

'No idea at all, Felix. Why?'

'Nothing. I'm just askin' anybody and everybody. You came in last night and went straight to your room and didn't stir all night. Ain't that right?'

The trap—where was it? Had he been seen? Felix was waiting, burning his scrutiny into him.

Vic asked, 'What was it you wanted to see me about?'

'I just remembered,' Felix said grimly, 'that you took Canary's side against Son. You was seen together outside the dance the night Son got murdered. Plumb chummy, you and Canary.'

164

'Ridiculous, and you know it!' Vic snapped.

'Maybe so. But I ain't forgot it. I could have you locked up again as a damned good prospect—don't forget that.'

Now the hole card would be turned over. Felix was driving at something. The threat just displayed was meant to back his play.

Felix fitted his fingers together. 'Let's get down to the nut-cuttin' of this cattle deal, Scott. Fact is, I've decided I'd like to see a little money. Could use it right now. You pay me half of the total. Ten thousand. That will bind the deal. Other half when you take delivery.' He added piously, 'That'll show both of us are dealin' in good faith.'

He means pay off or go to jail.

'It's a little unusual, Felix.'

'Who gives a goddam, long as I pass a thousand back to *you* at the same time? Money in hand for both of us. Hell, Stone and Chesman have got it to spare.' He added in spaced words, 'It would show you ain't just talkin' through your hat.'

A crooked cattle buyer would snap up the offer. Vic was a crooked cattle buyer. He said, 'I'm not one to turn down a thousand in hand. When you want to deal?'

'By this afternoon. Soon as the bank can telegraph Fort Worth and pay off on your draft.'

'That's a little fast for me. Why not Monday—day after tomorrow? I've got to write

165

up the terms and arrange for riders to move the herd.'

'Scott, why're you balkin' like a burro at a bridge?'

'You're talking big money, Felix. I've got to handle this in a way to keep my nose clean.'

Reluctantly, Felix said, 'All right. Monday. I want a check the bank will cash on telegraph authority from your Fort Worth bank. Then you get your thousand. Soon as I settle this Canary business, we'll round up the herd and you can take delivery and pay the balance. A deal?'

It had to be, Vic thought. A commission man who would make an under-table trade would be glad to get his rake-off fast. He looked at the triumphant snarl twisting Felix's face. 'It's a deal.'

A new contingent of dust-covered posse men pushed into the room and Felix transferred his attention to them. They had no news to report, and Felix began to outline orders for further riding. Vic pushed through them and headed back to the main street.

*   *   *

Amanda Forester wore a freshly ironed gingham dress and appeared to have spent a few painstaking minutes at her mirror just before Vic arrived. Her smile and charm were working with a vitality contradicting the night

166

of disturbed sleep. She greeted him with the easy friendliness of intimate conspirators and insisted that they take time to have coffee together before he saw Canary.

'Don't rush, Vic. He's back there and he will keep.' She added with engaging frankness, 'It's not every day I get to have coffee and a chat with an attractive man in my own house with none of the boarders around.'

He had questions for Canary Lenny burning him, but he forced himself to go along with her proffer of other mutual interests, whatever they were. He allowed his attention to register her attractiveness, the interesting lines of the well-fitted gingham, and the results of her time before the mirror.

'What a night!' Amanda said, as she served the coffee. 'First those Hebrons out there at headquarters, then you come in here with Canary Lenny, of all things! What on earth?'

'Puzzles me, too. I can only assume that Canary came to me because I befriended him.'

'Ann says she is almost positive that he didn't kill Son. She's made me believe that. But Felix has made up his mind.'

'Has anyone come here inquiring?'

'Not a soul. It's been amusing to me, Tully and all those men riding their fool heads off all over the country.'

'What have the Hebrons got against Canary? What was his trouble with them in the first place?'

167

A shadow went over her expression. 'I've never known, for sure. But I think Canary saw something, or knows something. Something that happened once—back when he was a horse wrangler for Tully—'

She failed to hide a slight tremble which shook her coffee cup.

Vic watched her closely without seeming to. 'This is a town full of mystery and distrust. So many seem to know things they don't want to tell.'

'This is the end of the earth, Vic. The Hebrons are the law and it's days to the civilized part of Texas. There's never any court, or any kind of trial here—unless it's somebody Felix and Ed want to take care of. Nobody would ever appear as a witness against any of the Hebrons, it's even impossible to get a jury. I'm surprised you'd even come out to this country to try to make a cattle deal.'

'I didn't know it was as bad as all this.'

'Well, they're stirred up now. Not only about Canary. But last night I gathered from a few remarks they're edgy over something else.'

'Yes? And what would that be?'

She hesitated, then looked levelly at him. 'They think there's some undercover law around, from somewhere outside.'

He knitted his brows as if to ponder that. 'Yes, I guess they would. After that Prez Duvall business.'

In a moment of silence, Amanda glanced at

a clock on the mantel, put down her cup and they stood at the same time. She lightly patted his forearm and said, 'You'll want to see Canary before my customers arrive. I'll stay and sort of keep an eye on the front door.'

He made his way down the corridor, and into Amanda's bedroom and across to the closed door of the storage cubicle. Canary Lenny sat on the edge of a cot. His strained face anxiously turned up as Vic closed the door behind him.

The youth blurted his torturing worry. 'They after me? They got any idea where I am, Mr. Scott?'

'No idea at all, Canary. You're safe.'

He questioned Canary again on the hacksaw, the voice at the jail window, the escape in the night. This brought nothing new. Canary had no idea who had passed the saw and instructed him to speed to Vic Scott's protection.

'What have the Hebrons got against you, Canary? What started your trouble with them in the first place?'

Canary doggedly shook his head. 'I ain't trustin' nobody on that.'

'Well, it's time you trusted me. You're in a hell of a pickle. If I'm going to help save your neck I'll have to know something. So you start talking, boy—you can either talk to me or I'll fix it so you will talk to Felix Hebron. Which do you want?'

Canary squirmed miserably.

'It was in Bitter Creek canyon that time. I happened to ride up on the rim when I was supposed to be somewhere else. They had a feller down there—and I *seen* it—!' Canary drew a deep breath. 'Godamighty, I seen what they did!'

'What fellow?'

'The stranger. His name, it was Cooper. Drew Cooper.' Canary stopped. Then, 'I knew they was a rough bunch and I'd seen Tully and Alto and Prez work over somebody they didn't like. But I never seen anything like *that.* I never saw nobody use a red-hot runnin' iron tryin' to make a man talk.' Sweat popped out on Canary. Vic felt moisture oozing from his own pores.

'Go ahead.'

'They finally backed off and shot him, all of them at once, like target practice. I heard later they thought Cooper was a spy of some kind, I dunno what.'

'Then they spotted you?'

'They seen somebody up there. I didn't get back in the brush in time. They thought it was me and tried to make me tell if I'd seen it. Tully, he held me and Chock and Alto twisted my arms. Then Prez broke my left arm with a rock. They told me to ride clear out of the country.'

'But you didn't leave?'

'Hell, there wasn't any place for me to go. I stayed down south at a Mexican sheep outfit till

170

I got mended. Worked around where I could. I thought it would blow over and got to slippin' into town once in a while. Son caught me once and beat me up. Never was anybody to take my side. Nobody 'cept Miss Lindsay. After she come, she was nice to me. She tried to get me to tell her what the trouble was, but I never told *nobody*.'

Vic mentally filed this for future consideration. He thought Canary had finished his story. But the dam in the youth's tongue had been broken and he started again. 'Then the other night, I saw that wagon come in.' His tone went low and intense. 'Tully, he was drivin' the team, and Chock and Alto and some of the others was ridin' alongside. Right after that was when everybody heard about Prez Duvall makin' that break.' Canary stopped.

'You didn't see where the wagon went?'

'Didn't hang around that long. But what I noticed, that wagon didn't just come from the ranch. It had been a long ways. Then, before they jumped me yesterday, I seen something else. I was holed up in a Mexican shack on the edge of town when I seen this Mexican woman go by on a mule. Woman that stays at the Hebron headquarters.'

He hesitated again and Vic prompted indifferently, 'Yes. What about her?'

'She had a bundle. Her name's Leona, used to be all kind of talk on the range—some said old Felix and Judge Ed used to keep her

171

around to lay her when they was all young—
that they had Mex bastards by her. Maybe Prez
Duvall, for one.'

'So you saw her ride by on a mule. What did
that mean to you, Canary?'

'Not what her ridin' a mule meant. She had
a bundle of laundry. Mule wasn't tired, so she
hadn't come from far. She come from yonder
way.' He gestured to somewhere beyond the
dark wall of the room.

Judge Ed's house was in that direction.
Kincaid, you made a mighty good guess. Vic felt
a stepped-up pumping of his blood. Tonight he
was due to enter Judge Ed's house, if Kincaid
succeeded in occupying Judge Ed with whisky
and cards at the Cactus Queen.

'Well, what did that mean to you, Canary?'

'Damn it, Scott! Meant to me she might of
been to see Prez. Somewhere not far from
here.'

'Canary, suppose I fixed it so you could
escape for good, clear out of the country. With
a good job back east and money to stake you
for a while. Would you be willing to testify in
court in some county back there, if it was a way
for you to get even with the Hebrons? A way to
send that bunch to the pen, and never get hurt
yourself?'

Canary considered. 'Might. I'd like to send
all them bastards to the scaffold for what I seen
'em do to Cooper that time and what they done
to me. If I was sure they couldn't run me down.'

172

Vic stood. He heard a rustle of sound beyond the door. The sound faded toward the hallway.

'You take it easy, now. I'm going to get you out of here, all safe and in good shape.'

'When, Mr. Scott?'

'It won't be long. You'll get word from me, or from Amanda Forester or Miss Lindsay. When you do, I want you to do exactly what you're told.'

He found Amanda waiting in the front room. 'Well, how did you and our star boarder make out?' she asked.

'Nothing new. I promised him I'd try to help him get out of the country. Are you willing to put him up another day or two?'

'Yes. I'll help. It's really a pleasure to be partners with you against the Hebrons.'

He tried to detect any veiled meaning in that and could not be certain. She placed her hand lightly on his arm. The gesture seemed intended to accentuate their partnership in this. He reached and patted her on the shoulder, a gesture meant for appreciation, or for his liking of her. He was thinking that here was a woman who had been through troubles, had weathered them with spirit, retaining her courage and inherent friendliness.

As he did this, her face tilted up to him. And in that moment, the light footsteps and the voice at the parlor's open door made them both guiltily pull back. Ann Lindsay stood there, her

173

words cut off in surprise, her features turning darkly perceptive.

She said stiffly, 'I beg your pardon.'

Amanda exclaimed airily, 'My goodness! Is it dinner time already?'

Ann's voice was coolly impersonal. 'Is Canary all right? Has anyone come?'

'Safe so far,' Vic said.

'Is it all right for me to talk with him?'

Vic studied her narrowly. 'About what?'

'Nothing in particular—just to encourage him.'

'I'd rather you wouldn't, just yet.'

'I've got to see about dinner,' Amanda cut in. 'The boarders will be trooping in here any minute.'

'Don't rush on my account,' retorted Ann. 'I'm not hungry.' She added, 'Sorry to have disturbed you two,' and her shoes clicked speedily down the corridor toward her room.

CHAPTER FOURTEEN

The moon made a slitted eye following him from the low tumble of clouds far west over the Chisos hills. He stayed crouched for long minutes, a shadow blended with other shadows, the yard bushes, the windmill, the corral fence. Judge Ed's darkened house stood there within a rock throw, its shuttered windows like dark hooded faces.

He could make out the full side of the house, a portion of the front porch to his right, and the near back corner. He waited with Indian patience. Finally, he detached himself from the cedar, crossed the open space, melted against the blackness of the house wall. He liked the dark protection there and was reluctant to move from it, but time was against him.

He examined the first window he came to and could find no telltale leak of light behind the tightly secured shutters. Feeling his way, he found the next window and pressed his ear against the timbers. This yielded no sound except the drone of his own pumping veins.

The windmill wheel fitfully stirred, crying in ghostly squeaks and groans from iron cogs and pump rod. Vic circled the steep-rising rear steps, straining to feel where each footstep would be placed. In spite of that he lightly grazed a tin can and it rolled a few inches on the packed earth. Something abruptly came to life on the high back porch. Vic slapped at his gun. A cat soared to the porch railing, settled its claws, and arched its black shape toward the intruder, its twin green embers showing like buttons on velvet. Vic waved his arm. The cat hurdled the steps and streaked toward the windmill.

At the corner, Vic gave his first attention to a checking-off study of each dark shrub and drooping mesquite on that side. Pinpoints of lights were visible in the distant town. He hoped that Kincaid and Judge Ed were amiably hitting it off over cards and bottle.

He moved to the nearest window and listened. He pressed his face flat against the lower edge and cupped his palms to shield his sight. The intensified blackness seemed unbroken at first, then the crack where the shutters met yielded one tiny sliver of yellow, hardly more than a short length of fine thread.

His breath caught and the doubt was gone. There was a light in that room. A light meant everything. It was no final answer, but it was the small sign for which this risk had been taken. Judge Ed normally would not leave a lamp burning in an empty house.

When the windmill stopped its uneasy whimperings for a moment, Vic listened against the shutters and thought he caught faint sounds within.

Then the stab of knowledge struck that whatever he had heard came from the back yard. There had been movement back there in the pitch darkness. Different from the cat, different from the windmill. Someone was there, outside the house.

He loosened his gun and inched along the wall, retracing his way. The dark shape of an animal came into view. He made it out as a mule, bareback, riderless, and reined to a tree. He knew it had not been there when he had crossed back of the house.

He heard a mumble of low voices. He moved

quickly into the straggly bushes at the corner and flattened himself against the boarding below the high back steps. His position immediately turned into a trap when the rear door flew open. A faint illumination came from within. He saw the outlines of a woman, retreating backward into the doorway. Her arms were raised defensively as she backed through and Vic recognized the Mexican woman, Leona, from Felix Hebron's headquarters.

She dodged and cried out as a heavy arm flashed in a shove at her. The man came all the way into Vic's line of sight and the arm belonged to Alto. The Hebron rider advanced as Leona retreated, and Vic could not move without exposing his presence.

Alto laughed and said a Spanish word. Leona uttered a sullen insult in reply. She attempted to turn at the top of the steps. Alto stalked her, and pushed her sprawling. She fell down the steps to the yard.

Leona scrambled to her feet, no more than six paces from where Vic had frozen against the porch siding.

Alto thudded down the steps. 'You wasn't supposed to come here again. Now you're goin' to get somethin'—'

He swung a heavy arm and propelled Leona into another backward retreat of short, unbalanced steps. Vic bent his body to prevent the contact but she floundered into him. In new

177

fright at this unknown presence, Leona squealed and whirled away.

'*Who is this?*'

At first, Alto seemed ignorant of her recoil from a man hidden in the darkness. The momentum of his rush continued unbroken and he slammed her to the ground. 'Now, old woman—'

In that moment, with Leona sprawled at his feet in a tangle of skirts, Alto discovered Vic. He stopped, paralyzed by surprise.

Vic made his spring to knock out Alto before he could be recognized. His fist jarred bone and all his knuckle bones seemed to shatter. Alto's last split-second dodge caught the blow on his temple instead of jaw. He swayed, but stayed on his feet, and Vic bore in with battering fists. Alto gave ground, but fought back. He swung a wild blow that caught Vic in the eye. Alto's breath rattled through his bloody mouth as he doggedly pushed the attack. He plunged at Vic head down and his massive shoulder powered Vic into a crash against the side of the house. His ribs seemed to cave in, his life to gush out. Alto worked his hand for the gun on his leg, and Vic charged him with both fists hammering. The rush carried them back toward the steps. Alto tripped over something soft on the ground, then both of them danced off balance to avoid Leona's prone shape. Alto tried to step backward over her. As he did, Vic smashed

178

with all his shoulder power in a chopping blow against the exposed taut muscle in the side of Alto's neck. The impact made the sound of a flat plank slapping water and Alto bellied heavily to the earth. He made a fishlike flop and bedded on his back, his head jerking in convulsions. Vic had fallen to his knees. He pushed away, intent on staying out of the light from the open back door.

Half blinded, he saw Alto fumble crazily for his gun beneath him. Vic tried with bruised, dead fingers to pull his own gun. His hand had no feeling.

He saw Leona stir and work at her thigh beneath her bunched skirts. Leona's arm raised. The faint gleam of reflected light touched the blade. Her arm plunged down. The blade vanished into Alto's broad stomach softness. He made a high whining sound like the racing windmill. His dark bulk pitched weakly. Then his hand quit searching for his gun.

Leona struggled to her feet. As Vic watched from the darkness, she fled in panic. A low voice called anxiously from inside. Then the back door slammed. All the light was gone. Woman, mule, Alto's still body, everything was swallowed in blackness.

The windmill creaked with maniacal glee in the mounting breeze. Vic staggered to sheltering foliage in the side yard. He heard an approaching horse and saw the rider emerge.

The man dismounted and unhurriedly walked up the front steps. His shape had a familiar outline to Vic's foggy senses but he was not sure until the man worked a key and opened the door. An inner light momentarily revealed him as Tully Forester.

Vic limped through the brush. He judged the time was near midnight. He found cover in a mesquite clump and lay down with his hundred hurts, the worst of them stabbing his ribs when he breathed. After a time he heard the sounds of galloping horses in the distant streets. He estimated an hour had gone by—time enough for Judge Ed to have been summoned, for Kincaid to have returned to the wagon yard. He arose and continued his walk, circling to come in from the back side. He reached the rear of the wagon yard pen, heard a movement in the trees, and worked out his gun with bruised and swollen fingers. A low whistle of identification sounded and Kincaid emerged.

'Come over here in the bushes.'

Vic followed him. Kincaid tried to make out Vic's features. 'You bunged up?'

'Plenty.'

'You know what you got to do, I reckon?'

'Yeah. Look for a fight.'

Vic smelled the whisky but Kincaid talked sober. 'It's got to be before the other man sees your face, whoever you pick. It's got to stand up when they check on it.'

'Any idea where, this time of night?'

'Maybe. The railroad construction camp. They got a saloon and them Irishmen and Eyetalians whoop it up all night on Saturday. There'll be fightin' drunks all around. Go pick you one.'

'That your horse back there?'

'Yeah. Take it. First, I want to know—he's there, all right, at Judge Ed's, ain't he?'

'He's there!' Vic said with satisfaction.

'Let's have it fast.'

Vic related it. 'So we can assume it's Prez inside. Alto was on guard and the Mexican woman came to see Prez. Maybe Judge Ed has been letting her in. But she ran into Alto. First he bullied her out of the house and then decided to rape her. Our job is cut out—hitting that place and taking Prez and getting him out of here before they move him.' He added, 'Your hunch was damned good.'

Kincaid said gloomily. 'Knowing where he is might be good, but nothing else. Better give you my end—we had a fine spree, me and Judge Ed and some of his town cronies. Then Tully Forester blew in, all in a wild lather. He called out Ed and a couple of Hebron men. I stayed around awhile and the word drifted back. Alto found stabbed to death outside Ed's house. They're looking for the Mex woman. The Hebron crew recognized the knife and it was the giveaway to her even if Prez tried to lie for her. But they know there was one hell of a fight. Their guess is some Mexican man, maybe

181

come with Leona. I figured it happened about like you've told it, and waited out here for you to show.'

'They'll be able to read the sign better in daylight.'

'They'll read it like Apaches. When they get a look at you, you've got to have an airtight story.'

'The ice is getting a little thin, Captain.'

Kincaid hiccoughed and wiped his mouth with his hand. 'Been thin under me all my life. But I hear it crackin' now ... Well, go out yonder and pick a fight and figure you got to get hurt and like it.'

Vic mounted the horse and rode west. He found the trail alongside the new roadbed and after a time the construction camp came into view. He rode through the scattering of shacks and tents to the lighted saloon. He dismounted and walked toward the front as two men staggered out to the street. Vic lurched near them, smacked one on the shoulder and said loudly, 'I can lick any two men in the camp!'

It was all that was needed. A roundhouse Irish fist sledge-hammered through the air. Vic ducked and jabbed at the flat-nosed face. Both men swarmed on him with exuberant whoops and the action sent his hurts into new stabbing pains. The saloon doors fanned with boisterous spectators emerging. Vic's two assailants powered him down. They floundered until he went limp, then the pair obligingly

182

disentangled themselves, stood, and roughly pulled him erect. One grunted, 'Calls for a snort—' and extracted a bottle. Vic swallowed a gulp and sloshed more of it on his shirt.

A new fight had broken out within the milling group, fed from inside the saloon, and this slugfest quickly became a free-for-all. A giant staggered to Vic, roaring, 'Let me have a lick at 'im!' Vic was engulfed in a new outbreak. The giant knocked him down with a round-house Vic caught on his shoulder, then drunkenly pulled him to his feet. 'Mike O'Malley at your service!' he roared.

Vic tried to match the roar. 'Vic Scott—comin' at you!' He smashed at the big face, then a dozen churning wrestlers unbalanced him and big Mike O'Malley hooked a leg behind him and shoved him sprawling. For a minute, Vic lay too hurt to move, hoping that the rioters wouldn't trample him.

Finally, the gang fight died and men straggled back into the saloon. Vic found himself one of four men stretched on the ground. He crawled erect and made his way to his horse.

He left the horse tied behind the wagon yard and limped toward the hotel. The town should have been dead to the world at three a.m. but lights burned in the saloons. Half blinded by the swelling of his eye, Vic crossed the lobby. The night clerk stared open-mouthed.

'What happened to you, Mr. Scott?'

'An Irishman named Mike O'Malley, at the construction camp,' Vic growled. The clerk sniffed at the whisky smell. Vic took the key and climbed the stairs to his room.

He let his dirty and bloodied clothing lie in a heap on the floor, the door unlocked and the key in the lock outside. Gingerly, he washed his bruises and cuts and held a cold cloth to his eye when he fell in bed. He only hoped they would not come for a few hours, giving him a little time for sleep and for the pain to subside.

*   *   *

They came when the sunlight first touched the windows and Tully led them. Behind him were Chock and the dark, stooped older rider he remembered seeing at Felix's house. They had their guns in their hands. Vic blinked as Tully threw back the covers. He found no hidden weapon, and then picked up Vic's clothes from the floor.

He grunted and showed the bloodstains to Chock and the man he called Blackie. Vic sat on the edge of the bed and felt of his half-closed eye.

Tully said, 'All right, Scott—where'd you run into a gatepost?'

'Those damned Irishmen at the railroad camp. Don't ever celebrate a Saturday night out there . . . What the hell you doing in here, Tully?'

184

A thoughtful frown had come to Tully's face. He snapped at Blackie, 'Ride out there and check it.'

Vic grumbled, 'And you can tell a giant named Mike O'Malley he near blinded me.'

Blackie left. Tully stuck Vic's .45 in his own coat pocket. 'Get up and dress, Scott. Put on these same bloody clothes.'

Vic stared inquiringly, and Tully said, 'You can ride out and tell Felix about it.'

CHAPTER FIFTEEN

Tully and Chock and two other Hebron men sat in the front room, lined in chairs along the wall like a silent jury hearing a case. Felix presided at the center table, a whisky bottle within reach instead of a gavel.

The hour was past noon. For a long time Vic had been left there while one man stood watch in the hallway. He had heard much coming and going of riders. Fragments of talk outside had included the names of Leona, Alto and his own.

Felix and Tully had been away; Vic had seen them pass the hall door but Felix had given him no more than a red-eyed, sour glance. Now Felix was back, and for the past fifteen minutes he had plied his cold and troubled questions.

He kept coming back to the subject of the cattle money, Vic's fight last night, and the

185

escape of Canary. Vic had replied with short, baffled answers, showing anger at being treated as a prisoner. More than once he had dangled the cattle payoff. Somehow, Felix had cooled on that.

'You didn't wire the Fort Worth bank,' Felix said accusingly. 'You're stallin' me. I don't like the smell of none of this.'

'Instead of doin' that, you went to the railroad camp, got drunk and had a fight. That don't sound like a man itchin' to close a big deal.'

'What the hell difference does that make?'

Felix shot an unexpected question. 'Where did you know Ann Lindsay before you landed here?'

Vic had to hesitate. Where was the trap?

'Who says I knew her before?'

'That ain't no answer.'

'You can leave her out of this. She's nothing to me. Nothing to do with this deal.' He stood, deciding to test their intentions. 'I've had enough of this performance. If you want to go ahead with our trade, Felix, this kangaroo court has to end right now.'

Tully flipped his coat edge from over his gun. Chock lifted the carbine from across his knees.

Felix twisted his scarred mouth. 'I doubt if there's goin' to be a deal. If you'd wanted to trade as big as you talk, you'd a wired Fort Worth yesterday. Found out at the telegraph

186

station you didn't.'

'I intended to make the payoff tomorrow.'

'So I wired for you.' Felix craftily closed one eye. 'To Stone and Chesman."Telegraph bank authorization immediately for ten thousand to close desirable purchase." Signed Victor Scott.'

Vic had the sensation of the floor caving in under him. He tried to keep his expression blank as he waited for disaster. Everyone watched him and waited. He was thoroughly covered at Stone & Chesman, he thought. Damn it, they knew in Fort Worth a man's life was at stake out here.

Finally, he had to ask, 'Well, what did they say?'

'They didn't answer,' Felix muttered. 'Not a damned word.'

Relief pumped inside Vic. No answer was better than anything they could have said.

But Felix saw it differently. 'Why wouldn't they shoot back an answer, Scott? Half a day and all night they've had. Ain't your home outfit speakin' to you?'

'There could be a dozen reasons. Maybe the office was closed. Today's Sunday. You had no business forging my name to a telegram. You want to crumb the deal?'

Felix took a drink from the bottle. During that pause, horses galloped into the yard. The man watching from the hallway returned, ushering in Blackie and another arrival. Vic was startled at sight of the stooped figure of

Doc Flayhorn.

Felix cut them short by snapping, 'Spill it, Blackie!'

'He was at the railroad camp, all right.' The dark-skinned rider motioned at Vic. 'There was a free-for-all fight. Most of them out there are still groggy drunk. But somebody remembered him. He tried to whip their champion, name of O'Malley.'

Felix and Tully looked disappointed.

To Flayhorn, Felix commanded, 'Look him over, Doc.'

The veterinarian put down his bag. He frowned unhappily. 'Sit yourself, Scott.' Flayhorn made an examination of Vic's bruised face. He poked at his ribs, noticing Vic wince, and examined Vic's bruised right hand.

'It was a hell of a battle, whoever it was,' Flayhorn mumbled. 'What did you fetch me out here for, Felix? What you expect me to find out?'

'I wanted you to figure if it looked like Alto done it—that's what I want. Would he have got all that in little saloon fracas with them railroaders?'

'Now how the hell would I know where he got it?'

'You ought to have some idea.'

'Alto had some cracked fingers. Took something hard, like this one's eyesocket, maybe. Shirt front bloody. So was Alto's mouth.' Flayhorn pulled on his chin. 'Scott,

188

other day, when I gave you those sleeping pills, did you root in my desk drawer in my office?'

Vic got to his feet. Tully stood and moved toward him. Vic said, 'I've had enough of this kind of palaver.'

Tully smashed an open hand into Vic's chest, knocking him back into the chair. Flayhorn cautioned, 'Careful, Tully. He may have some cracked ribs.'

Tully glanced at Chock, back to Flayhorn. 'What about sleeping pills?'

'I gave him a supply. He came to my office—'

'Chock had a big sleep,' Tully said, thinking hard. He worked his cigar and looked down at Vic. 'Chock never passed out from whisky before in his life till Scott showed up the other day and poured him a drink at the Bitter Creek shack—'

Chock muttered, 'Sure wasn't ordinary whisky, Tully.'

Vic watched Felix. The boss Hebron fitted his calloused fingertips together and spoke almost sadly, 'Tully, you reckon we got us another *Drew Cooper* on our hands?'

*   *   *

Noontime passed, and the sun moved its slant to the high west side of the Hebron headquarters. For two hours Vic sat alone in the room with only a Hebron man lounging on watch in the hallway.

189

Doc Flayhorn came from the back of the house, picking his teeth, and Tully followed him. Flayhorn opened his bag, saying to Tully, 'Might as well fix him up, long as I'm here.' Tully watched without comment as Flayhorn had Vic strip to the waist. He rubbed liniment over the bruised rib patches, wrapped Vic's chest tightly with heavy cloth, then applied ointment to his swollen eye. Neither Tully nor Flayhorn bothered to make answers to Vic's few attempts to talk and he gave it up. They departed and the afternoon dragged on.

When Vic heard the approaching horses, he moved slightly to be able to see the front yard from the window. With a sinking awareness of his final entrapment, he realized why they had been waiting.

The new arrivals were Sheriff Arch Moon and Ann Lindsay.

He saw that she wore riding clothes, and before she dismounted she made a friendly wave to Felix and the others on the porch. Moon came around and politely helped her from the saddle. After a time of talk on the porch, Ann came hesitantly from the hallway into the room. Felix, Tully, Moon and Chock trooped after her.

She paused and met Vic's glance, raised her head a quarter of an inch, and proceeded to a chair without speaking. He saw her color slightly heighten, and the rise and fall of her breast in quickened breathing. The men seated themselves; Felix fixed her with a drooping smile which she returned with a small tightening of her lips. She raised her brows in inquiry.

'Reason we sent for you, we want to know something,' Felix began. He paused to fortify himself with a lift of the bottle. 'We want to know about this man Vic Scott, right in front of him. He blowed in here and the first night he took you to the dance. Ain't that kinda funny, you and Son about to get married, and all?'

Ann folded her hands. She seemed to have complete composure, but the touch of color still showed in her cheeks. 'Why, I don't know, Felix. I just did it on the spur of the moment. I guess to make Son jealous. But he's more interested in Amanda than me.' She looked across at Vic and he thought, *That part she really means.*

'I figured maybe you knew him back somewhere. You come from Fort Worth. So does he. You wouldn't mind helpin' ole Felix on a little somethin', would you, hon? If you had ever run across this Scott before?'

'Of course, Felix. Anything I can do.' She turned again for a full look at Vic across the room. She seemed to be attempting to analyze the situation into which she had been brought.

She murmured to Felix, 'What's the trouble here? Is he—does this have to do with something I should know about?'

'Has to do with Son. Has to do with Canary

191

Lenny. Has to do with Alto getting stabbed to death. Not that Alto was anybody we'll miss much, and the same goes for Leona.' He bent forward, tightening his fists on the table. 'Give it to me straight, girl. If you ever knew him before, I want to know who in hell he *is*.'

Wonderingly, Ann said, 'Why he's a cattle buyer, isn't he? That's all I know about him, Felix.'

'Damn it, I asked you, did you ever hear of him before he hit Angelo?'

She surveyed Felix's strained features calmly after that outburst. Vic saw that her folded hands had tightened and turned white at the knuckles. *Is it a trap for me—or for her?*

Ann made a quick sidewise look at Vic, then about at the tensely staring Hebron men. She spoke earnestly to Felix. 'I wasn't going to say anything about it and it really doesn't matter, so far as I can see. We never met before he came to town, but I *had heard him* spoken of in Fort Worth. I've been so terribly upset, about Son—'

Her voice faltered. She dusted Vic with another glance from her dark eyes. *She's making it up as she goes.* He waited with his insides knotted to see what her lie was leading to.

The others watched her in strained expectancy. Felix waited with his mouth wetly open.

'Yeah, go on, girl—what had you heard?'

192

Ann said honestly, 'I never knew him personally. I only knew that he was a cattle buyer. Quite a man with the ladies, they said. And that his reputation wasn't so good.'

'With the ladies?' Felix purred.

She shook her head. 'Maybe that, too. But I meant as a cattle buyer. That he was one who would pull a shady deal, only his company had never caught him at it yet. I heard he had served a prison term in—in California . . .'

Ann stopped and the silence hung. Vic coldly stared at her. But his blood surged warmly inside him, saying, *You've likely just saved my life.*

Felix cleared his throat. 'A crook, huh?'

'Now that's all I know, Felix.'

Felix sat back and chewed his lower lip. He looked morosely at Tully and at Vic and around at the others.

'Well, I reckon that's about what we wanted to know. With you and Son bein' the way you was, you're like one of the family, Ann. Fine, truthful girl, and I appreciate your comin' out here with Arch. We just got a little problem, and you've helped us clear it up—'

He stood and at his motion Ann preceded them from the room. She walked in front of Vic, not looking at him. Felix put his arm about her shoulder as they vanished in the hallway.

After a time, through the window, he saw Ann and Sheriff Moon ride toward town. Felix and Tully returned to the room. Felix said

193

jovially, 'Damn me, forgot you ain't et, Scott. Come on back and I'll have cook fix you something before you start for town.'

'Is the kangaroo court ended?'

'Didn't mean to rile you. You just follow up on that payoff tomorrow and we'll close the deal. Just curious, but what did they catch you doin' in California?'

Vic gruffly replied, 'A little mining stock scheme went sour.'

Tully was not as jovial as Felix. He took the dead cigar from his mouth. 'I've got one thing to tell you, Scott. Stay away from Amanda.'

Mockingly, Vic drawled, 'A man takes his pleasure where he can find it.'

'If I catch you at it, it won't be pleasure.'

Felix mumbled almost with a tone of admiration, 'A known crook and a ladies' man, huh?'

* * *

He rode a Hebron horse and reached town at dusk. No signal showed itself in Kincaid's window. He left the horse at the hotel stable and walked along the sidewalk before the frame fronts. When he was sure no one followed him, he dodged into a dark alley, out the other end, and came to the trees back of the wagon yard. The worry persisted that Captain Kincaid might be sleeping off his whisky while their last thin covering of safety

194

was coming to pieces. He climbed the dark outside steps and took out the key Kincaid had given him.

As the door swung open, he made out Kincaid sitting up in bed in his union suit with his two revolvers leveled on him. Kincaid grunted. Vic said, 'Thought you might be asleep.'

'Was, but not that sound asleep.'

Vic told him of forcibly being taken to the Hebron headquarters and of the scene there.

Kincaid commented, 'That hotel woman was battin' for you, looks like. I don't understand her, any more than you do. Damn it, we got to nail her down! You never searched her room yet, have you?'

'Haven't had the chance.'

'Well, you got one now.' Kincaid rolled a smoke. A match flare briefly lighted his drawn, gray-stubbled jaws. 'She came back to town. Then I saw her and Amanda drive off in a buggy, all Sunday dressed. You know where they went? To *church*! I sneaked up to a window to make sure. Damned if they ain't in the choir, singin' their fool heads off with a lot of other dressed-up women. A loco town this is.'

Vic agreed. 'I'm ready to make the big try and get out.'

'Well, let's see. I kept an eye on Judge Ed's house. Nothing unusual happened. If it was Prez, he's still there. The Mexican woman has disappeared. Kept my other eye on Amanda's house to make sure it hasn't leaked out about Canary. Scott, we're square against it. Time's run out and we got to make our move.'

'When, Captain?'

'Tomorrow night. Not later. They're goin' to have you across a stump on that cattle money. They're apt to find out about Canary any time, maybe find Leona, too. She could have recognized you fighting Alto. The clock is tickin' out on us.' He stalked across the room. Vic heard the cork pulled and turned his head away. Kincaid coughed and barefooted back to the edge of the bed.

'While the women're at church, suppose you look through Ann Lindsay's room. I'd like to have her tabbed one way or another. She's one that can ruin us if we ain't guessed right.'

'She backed me with a neat lie to Felix. A known crook, she said. That was top-grade recommendation to that crew.'

'Smart. Damn tricky, too. Son Hebron's girl taking up for a stranger for no reason that makes sense. Tell me the truth, Scott, you made time with her since you been here?'

'No. Not that way.' Vic frowned. 'Actually, I think she figures I'm making a play for Amanda. She showed she didn't like that.' He added, 'Tully likes it even less.'

'Well, she's an unknown to us, and an unknown in this kind of business ain't healthy. You take a look at her room while they're

196

churchin' and lemme have my nap. I was up all night and all day, too. After a while I got to get back in the brush and watch Ed Hebron's house. We got to know if they try to move our boy out of there tonight.' He thought of something and added sourly, 'You better keep your mind on that rich gal in Austin and stay clear of Amanda. Wouldn't be worth it if Tully caught you.'

Vic bristled. 'When in hell do you think I'd have time?'

Kincaid chuckled appreciatively. 'Would have to be on the run, wouldn't it?'

*   *   *

Vic found Amanda Forester's front door unlocked, slipped inside, and first visited Canary in his cubby-hole hiding place. Canary worriedly wanted to know when Scott was going to get him out of there. Vic told him, 'Right soon, now.' He returned to the corridor, silently moved to the built-on wing, and twisted the doorknob of Ann's room. He adjusted the shades and curtains, then touched a match to a lamp. In its low-turned light he began a systematic examination, putting down his feeling of reluctance at rooting through her clothing and personal belongings. Her wardrobe and other possessions appeared to be in meager supply. The drawers were devoid of the trinkets and keepsakes a woman would be

197

expected to have tucked away. He did not find a single letter saved, no item to suggest a link either to her past or to the Hebrons. Then, in the bottom drawer of the dresser, beneath neatly folded clothing, his fingers touched a small leather case. It was locked, and he forced the lid with the blade of his pocket knife. He drew out a thin square-shaped packet wrapped in tissue. He removed the covering and stared at what the faint light revealed.

The folds of paper had covered a small photograph and a tiny circular object wrapped tightly and separately. His fingers recognized what was within even before he finished untwisting the paper. It slipped from his grasp and fell to the rug. He picked it up and the lamplight touched its yellow gold sheen.

A wedding ring.

He held it near the lamp and examined the inner side, and found the small engraving: *Ann and Drew.*

He brought the small photograph into the weak touch of light and stared at the faded likeness of a face he remembered from the past. As recognition came, his lips soundlessly formed the name of his Texas Ranger friend of other years. Drew Cooper.

For a moment he let the revelation etch into his mind, clearing so many things. Her play to Son and the other Hebrons, the small gun in her bag, her protection of the crooked cattle buyer before Felix.

He rewrapped the ring and the photograph as he had found them and returned them to their original place. He extinguished the lamp, rearranged the shades and curtains, and slipped into the hallway. He made the turn in the dark corridor.

He had reached a position just outside Amanda's bedroom when he heard the sound at the front.

CHAPTER SIXTEEN

The intrusion came so quickly that Vic had no time to do more than freeze against the wall. A light illuminated the head of the hallway and a voice called roughly, 'Amanda! Amanda!—I want to talk to you . . . You here?'

Before Vic could move, Tully Forester appeared with a lamp in his hand. Their recognition of one another was instantaneous. Tully stiffened and made a grunting sound of surprise. He placed the lamp on a small hall table with his left hand and flicked his right. His gun whipped up, covering Vic. Fast as his draw was, Vic matched it instinctively and his own gun was leveled on Tully.

They stood still for seconds. Suspicion twisted Tully's features, then understanding turned his expression to hatred. This passed, as the seconds stretched, and Tully deliberately lowered his gun.

199

Tully mumbled, 'I don't aim to kill you, or her either. It's not worth us killin' one another over. Put down your gun, Scott.'

Tully's attention stabbed to the closed door beyond Vic. He began a slow walk forward. Vic stepped in front of the door.

'You're not going in there, Tully.'

'I'm goin' in there.'

'You're not opening this door.'

'I'm openin' it.' Tully kept his slow advance. Now his tautness had subsided and his body drooped with the pain of his discovery. 'I'm goin' to see her. I just want one look at her, and I want her to have to look me in the eye, and if she's got her clothes on or if she's got 'em off it don't make any difference.'

'She's not yours any longer, Tully. She's not your wife and this is not your house.'

Tully was within an arm's reach now. 'Stand aside, Scott. I've caught you two, just like I suspicioned. I'm going to look her in the eye, then I'm going to slap her clean across the room and then I'm spreadin' the word in every saloon that she's just a goddam whore. That's the way I'm gettin' even.'

'It's not that way, Tully.' *Canary Lenny, for God's sake don't sneeze, don't even breathe.*

Tully was a man with his insides knotted in the tortures of a lost possession and his pride was in rebellion. Vic said earnestly, 'Tully, get this now—she's not here. She and Ann are at the church. You can go there and see for

200

yourself.'

Tully shook his head in numb disbelief. 'I know where she is. She's hunkered up in there under the bed covers, scared to death—'

'If you'll just wait in the front parlor a little while you'll see her and Ann walk in dressed up, from church.'

'No.' Tully stubbornly shook his head again. 'You're not foolin' me. If you knew she was at church, *you* wouldn't be comin' out of her room. So you're lyin'. Stand aside.'

He could stand aside and let Tully have his look. Then Tully would want to settle his last shred of suspicion. He would spot the door to the small storeroom, stalk to it for a look inside, fling it open and be greeted by the sight of the terrified Canary Lenny.

'You owe her that much respect, Tully. Both her and me. If she and Ann don't come in from church in thirty minutes, then prove me a liar and take the house apart for all I care. Just do your former wife the small respect any woman deserves—'

He knew his argument was vague, but Tully was almost listlessly lost in his own hurts. He turned slowly and Vic followed him. Each step away from Canary's hiding place seemed to Vic as that much safety gained. As they reached the stand where the lamp stood, Tully paused, pulled his gun, and placed it beside the lamp. 'You put your gun here with mine,' he said thickly. 'Whichever way it turns out, I don't

201

want to lose my head and hurt you, Scott, and I don't want you to lose yours and hurt me.'

He twisted his head in challenge. It sounded all right, and it didn't, but after a hesitation Vic placed his gun beside Tully's. 'That's fair enough.'

He never knew whether Tully deliberately set the trap, or whether Tully's brain snapped in the heat of his jealousy. Halfway across the room, Tully stopped. His shoulders hunched and his legs strangely stiffened. Tully made a deep chest growl, whirled, and charged. Vic sensed the attack was coming only a split second before Tully struck, and his memory shrilled a warning of the hidden knife Tully wore. The Hebron foreman swarmed upon him in a ferocity of madness. Desperately, Vic tried to throw up his arms in protection. The crash of their bodies shot fiery pains through Vic's injured ribs. The struggle, part stumbling clinch, part pumping fists and knees, carried them over the room. A chair crashed, a small table toppled. From his sea of pain, Vic pushed Tully back with an open-handed shove into the distorted face and followed that with an explosive fist into the side of Tully's head. Tully staggered back and fell to the floor. Vic's knees wobbled. He had the sensation of a new and different kind of hurt in his side. All at once he went down as if a rope had jerked his feet from under him. The room whirled, and somewhere in its turning he saw the knife on the rug, with the moist crimson streak on its blade.

He realized that he was pressuring his left fist hard into his ribs beneath his jacket. The burn there was different from all the rest. A wetness seeped through, sticky against his pressing knuckles.

He saw Tully raise himself and shake his head. On his hand and knees, Tully began a fast crawl toward the knife. His hand reached and caught its handle, and he propelled himself across the rug toward Vic.

With his left fist pressured into the moist burning spot, Vic willed himself to move, to meet the oncoming man, knowing that Tully was on his way to finish the job. Limply, Vic's right arm gave way beneath him. There was no strength left to support his weight. Tully came on, breathing loudly, crazily mumbling. He pushed along the rug with the knife gripped in his fingers.

The shot from the hallway door blasted the dim room apart and two shots quickly behind the first prolonged the turbulence. Tully was flung halfway about by the .45 slugs. Vic twisted to better see the crouched figure with the gun.

Bent forward and staring, with the smoking sixgun in his hand, Canary Lenny faced toward Tully. Amanda's ex-husband would never know the answer to his night of suspicion. His right arm lay outstretched with the knife a few inches beyond his fingers.

Canary looked with awe from Tully to the

gun in his hand. 'My God, I killed *Tully Forester*!'

Vic fought a consuming weakness and raised to his knees, then erect, pressing his fist into his side. 'The other gun, Canary—on the table—get it—'

Canary brought the Colt and Vic took it, barely able to hold its weight.

'I heard the ruckus,' Canary said through chattering teeth. 'I knew it was Tully and I thought I was done for. I slipped out, and seen those guns, and then he was comin' at you—'

Vic muttered, 'You did just fine, Canary.' He tried to tell Canary they must hurry, that they must be gone before sounds of the shots brought someone to the house, and that he was losing blood from the stab wound in his side. The words played out and he could only jerk his head toward the door. He stumbled to the porch. Canary hurried, took Vic's arm, and guided him into the darkness.

Later, Vic had only blurred memory of wandering through the night. He remembered repeating to Canary, 'Keep away from the lights.'

At some point, while they rested, Canary said, 'Only place I can think of is the Izaguirre house, it's the last shack on the back road in the Mexican settlement. The people went to Mexico, nobody there—'

Sometime in the night they came upon a dark 'dobe and Canary worked at the door.

Canary's hands guided him to a cot, and he dimly knew when a flame touched candle, and later he thought he heard low voices.

He became aware that hands were forcing his clenched fist away from the moist spot in his shirt. The face of the Mexican woman, Leona, floated into his vision, with the white-eyed Canary beside her. Seeing Vic's eyes open, Canary said, 'She was hidin' here, too, Mr. Scott—she's kin of the Izaguirres—'

Leona hissed for silence and began working at Vic's blood-matted shirt. He closed his eyes against pain and weakness, and was barely conscious when Leona plugged the blood seepage and bandaged the small black slit.

* * *

Captain Kincaid stirred restlessly and tried to hold on to the needed shield of sleep. The flurry of sounds, alien to the night, drifted in the window. He struck a match and looked at his watch. Just two hours since Vic Scott had left. There appeared to be an undue number of horses and people on the move. He went over and peered from the window.

The night sounded like trouble, smelled like trouble. He dressed, strapped on his sixguns, and soon walked along the main street toward the first lights. From other men, aroused by the disturbance, he heard the news. He fell in with a group of the curious who strung out in a walk toward Amanda Forester's house.

Several horses were tied outside the yard. The front door stood open. Men were coming and going, and a few stood talking on the porch. As Kincaid waited with the spectators, men carried a blanket-wrapped body from the house and lifted it across a horse that had been led to the steps. One took the horse away as two others walked and steadied its burden.

Kincaid watched from the back of the silent group. Sheriff Arch Moon and Deputy Sam Tabor came toward them. Moon announced, 'I need as many of you men as have got horses to ride as a posse. Them as can go, get your mounts and rifles.'

A few of them responded. One detained Moon and asked, 'Was it her that killed him, Arch?' Kincaid, listening, casually began rolling a wheatstraw without a grain of tobacco spilling.

'No. Both women were at church. Nobody was in there but Tully and the man that killed him.'

'Any idea who, Arch?'

'Maybe. Waitin' for Felix and his men. Ed's already here. Whoever it was, he and Tully had a mighty fight before Tully got three bullets poured into him.'

Moon plodded back toward the house and Tabor left with the posse men. The spectators began to drift back toward the saloons, Kincaid among them.

He worked his mind on the question of where Vic Scott would go to hide, and could think of no safe place. He took it for granted that Scott would be hunted by the Hebron crowd, on general principles. Assuming that, then he had to concede that Scott hereafter could not show himself anywhere in Angelo where he might be seen. Bleakly, as he trudged toward the main street, Kincaid thought the case finally had gone to hell completely and that there was not one chance in a hundred he and Scott could organize their final move against Prez Duvall. For a moment, he was tempted to try to pass word to the unknown federal man, Paul & Co. But that would take time. And orders had been given that this was to be done only as a last resort. Well, thought Kincaid, if they didn't have their backs to the wall now, they were damned close to it . . .

He entered the Angelo Saloon and joined the line-up where the talk hummed on Angelo's latest sensation. Kincaid toyed with the shot glass before downing the burn. He wondered how it had happened. Had Tully trailed Vic and jumped him? Had Vic managed to get Canary out of there? Evidently so, else everybody would know by now that the jail-breaker had been found in Amanda's house.

He waited, listening to the nervous comment around him. He bought a quart bottle of whisky and worked it under his coat. He cut across the alley and into the mesquites bordering the wagon yard. He left the bottle in his room, found no sign that Scott had been there, and departed again by the back stairs. He began his long, circling route and came in to the south of Judge Ed's house. Whatever else might be going on tonight, he clung to stubborn purpose. He had to keep watch through the lonesome hours, to be certain that Prez Duvall was not moved from his hole-up. He settled himself into the dark covering of cedar brush. The night wore on, like so many others of this kind of patient waiting which had formed the pattern of his life.

Nothing happened at Judge Ed's house.

Before the first dawn would lighten the brush, he began his retreat, made the far circling return, and came into the main street as the sky lightened to a weak gray. Lamps still burned in the Cactus Queen, the Angelo Saloon, and the hotel lobby. Horses drooped at the rails. In the Angelo, and again in the Cactus Queen, he heard the rumors from the all-nighters, but learned nothing new. Felix and his men were out in force, looking for a certain man—and nobody had his name for sure.

At each bar, Kincaid downed a whisky nightcap, then tiredly returned to his room. In his union suit, and with both guns arranged beside his pillow, Kincaid decided to have one more, just for going to sleep on. He opened the bottle he had bought at the saloon and downed one, and then another for good measure and gentler going to sleep. He blew out the lamp flame and crawled into bed. Its softness felt good to old and weary bones, and he slept.

*   *   *

The graying new day also touched the last adobe shack on the weedy back street of the Mexican settlement. A trickle of the Monday dawn fingered past the window shade and finally brought the outlines to focus within the silent room.

Vic did not want to open his eyes. His mind slowly stirred with memory of the night. In his first awakening, he feared any movement would return the onslaught of pain.

He worked his right hand experimentally, loosening the bruised fingers. They touched warm steel and he nursed the butt of his Colt which he remembered ordering Canary to place under the covering quilt.

He lay on his back with his eyes closed.

Without seeing, he realized the room had lighted and that dawn had come. He listened, but heard no sounds of Canary or Leona.

Slowly, he caused his left eyelid to flutter for his first veiled look. The gray image he saw closed it tight again. His mind fought against the admission because it was unbelievable.

He forced himself to open both lids barely enough to prove that there was no denying what he had seen. Through the thin slit of gray

209

he looked at the man in the chair and the full knowledge flooded him. Worse than the stab wound.

The man sitting in the straight chair was Deputy Sam Tabor. Tabor sat with his elbows on his knees, bent forward, absently toying with something in his hands. Vic's veiled study followed down Tabor's arms to the object. What he recognized there in Tabor's hands seemed to strip from him the last small shred of protection.

Tabor was toying with Vic's thin canvas shoulder holster and its snub-nosed gun, the potent toy that had killed Son Hebron.

Somehow, they had tracked it down. And as if the sickening jolt of that were not enough, Vic caught sight of something else. A dim shape filled the other corner of the room, almost blotted out in a chair against the wall.

Canary Lenny.

Canary also sat with his head down, his chin hung on his chest, with his mouth open and his eyes closed. His hands rested in his lap, bound together with the short chain length of brass handcuffs.

A change in Vic's breathing, or the veiled eyelids moving, must have caught Tabor's notice. Tabor straightened and his fingers quit their idle playing with Vic's shoulder gun. Tabor raised his head.

Vic closed his eyes and heard Tabor stand, and Vic slid his hand an inch under the quilt.

His fingers closed on the butt of his heavy Colt. He lifted it, opened his eyes full, and the gun muzzle made a protruding point in the bed quilt, directed straight at Tabor.

The movement caught the swarthy deputy with the shoulder holster still occupying both hands in front of him.

In the first two seconds, Vic thought the deputy was going to drop the canvas holster and try to draw. Vic flung off the quilt with his left hand. Gritting against the pain, he twisted to his side and brought the Colt up uncovered.

Tabor stood motionlessly and it was too late for the gamble. With a corner of his mouth pulled grim, he stared at the muzzle of the gun.

He watched Vic's trigger finger. Vic tightened the pressure.

Tabor dragged his gaze off the finger, past it to Vic's eyes, and held them. His expression showed chagrin at allowing himself to be trapped, plus a gleam of healthy fear that the trigger finger was going to press a fraction too hard.

He smiled awkwardly and his voice came out strained. Tabor said, 'Don't pull that trigger, Scott. I'm Paul and Co.'

CHAPTER SEVENTEEN

Vic licked his lips, his ears rang, the gun in his hand tried to flutter.

'I work for a man named Gilbert. His first

211

name is Rufus.'

Tabor murmured, 'I knew it as Angus.'

'Your firm's headquarters are in Kansas City.'

'No, Washington, D.C.'

'The hide-out gun you hold?'

'Came in the mail.' Tabor's lip twitched. 'Thought the owner might need it again, it did such an efficient job for him before. I damned sure needed to get rid of it.'

'Your company know of a lease hunter in town?'

'His name is Kincaid.'

Vic experimentally brought his feet around to the floor and found he could sit without increasing the hurt. 'You damn people take your time making new acquaintances.'

'You took your own damn sweet time getting the pressure off that trigger. I thought you were going to dent my badge.'

Vic grinned as admiration welled up inside. 'Consider my hat off to you. I don't see how you've done it.'

Tabor shrugged. 'Sometimes I don't either. Hasn't been easy.' He came to the bed. Vic extended his hand and shook with Tabor. Canary was taking them in with a baffled expression.

Vic asked, 'The handcuffs?'

'Just precaution. Played my role with Canary when I slipped in.'

'Can you get him out of earshot?'

'There's a back room.' Tabor directed Canary out ahead of him, then returned and pulled a chair to the bed. 'My time's short, Scott. Officially, I'm searching the Mexican houses. Gambled that Canary would head for the shack of his friends, the Izaguirres, and that you might be hibernatin' with him. I knew Leona had come here. My informant is a Mexican who's doing a similar job for his Foreign Department. I can't risk too much time in here.' He added quietly, 'You're in big trouble.'

Vic groped in his mind for a place to begin. One concern pushed itself to the front of all others. 'Ann Lindsay—is she safe?'

'I suppose so.' Tabor looked genuinely puzzled. 'She and Amanda are in the clear on last night. They were at church.'

He doesn't know, Vic thought. She had guarded her secret well. 'Listen, Tabor—she testified for me in front of Felix. That may have burned her bridges. If they're after me, they'll remember that. If I'm not who I pretend to be and they know it, then Felix knows Ann Lindsay lied for me. I want her prepared to disappear *fast.*' The worry mounted in his mind. 'It could be too late now.'

'What's her connection?'

Tabor didn't know and Vic started to tell him. Then he hesitated. For some reason, he wanted to be the first to talk with her. It was a personal and private thing, and now filled with more danger than she could have expected.

'Did you know Drew Cooper?' he asked Tabor.

'Only heard of him. The U.S. Marshal's headquarters in Texas imported me from California for this one, complete with a new name and an airtight fugitive record. Why?'

'You ever meet his widow?'

Tabor shook his head. He suddenly stared at Vic, then his lips pursed. 'Good God! You don't mean it?'

'I want to talk to her first. Can you get her here?'

Tabor considered. 'How about an anonymous note, delivered by Kincaid? I wouldn't want her to know I was behind it.'

'Make it soon, will you? Now, what do I need to know?'

'Felix wants you. Somebody thought they saw you going toward Amanda's last night. The theory is Tully broke in on a bedroom situation, even if Amanda was at church. Felix wants you bad, for that and other suspicions. I'm afraid they have you tabbed, or at least they consider there've been too many incidents involving you since you hit Angelo. I don't know everything—I'm not in on all Felix's private ideas, just what leaks to me through Moon.'

'Next thing—is Prez Duvall at Judge Ed's?'

'That has to be a guess. I'd say yes, from indications. Son had been going there nights.

214

Doc Flayhorn was in and out. I think they hid Prez at the Bitter Creek range camp first, then made Judge Ed take him in to be closer to Doc Flayhorn.'

'You in a position to help us pull that off?'

Tabor shook his head. 'Afraid I can't uncover yet, Scott. I'm to protect the foothold I've managed to get here and my job is different, you know. My people want a case built on the Mexican cattle steal, the federal issue on that, and they want evidence put together for a federal conviction of the killer of Drew Cooper.'

'I've got a witness for that. Canary Lenny.'

'Figured so. I'd like for you to get him out and keep him on ice for us. Our jobs may overlap but my orders are to stick to what status I've gained out here. Prez is a state case at the moment and will have to be your problem. I'll help to what extent I can, without showing my hand.'

'All right.' Vic tried to think it out. 'We've got to make our move tonight. My time's run out. If they move Prez we'd have to start all over. Can you do this—manage to get word to Kincaid that he'll have to set it up, how we go for Prez. He'll have to organize that and our means of a getaway with a crippled prisoner. With Judge Ed, too, if we can haul him in at the same time. We've got him on a solid charge of harboring the fugitive. I'd like Felix—but that's expecting too much luck.' He thought of the

215

odds and added moodily, 'Kincaid should lay off—'

He stopped and Tabor knowingly finished for him, 'Whisky.'

Vic doggedly shook his head. 'But he can hold it—'

Tabor alertly studied him. 'Scott, you're feverish. Canary says you caught only a flesh stab, but you need a doctor. Still, I don't know how that could be managed in this town.'

'I feel strong enough and I'm bandaged like a mummy.'

'Well, this will send your fever higher. Kincaid was seen buying a bottle in the saloon last night. The pressure will be building up on him all day.'

With Vic's burning pulse throbs there came a kind of perverse sense of loyalty for the old Ranger. 'He's able to plan it.'

'But what if he's three sheets?' Tabor insisted. 'You're gambling your life, man!'

Vic took a few paces on the bare floor, testing his legs. 'Let's start with this: can you create some kind of diversionary search somewhere, say around midnight? Can you go so far as to arrange for a wagon and fast team? That's for carrying Prez and Ann Lindsay and anyone else we wind up with when we hit. Figure for me the best trail out that will be in cover and still lead us back to the Sweetwater road after we get some distance behind us.'

Tabor agreed, and then said, 'Now I've got

216

to move, Scott. Quicker I report no signs in the Mex settlement, easier to steer them away from here. The peons will keep quiet, even if they spot you. They've been bullied by the Hebrons for years. Some of Leona's kin have already arranged for her—she's hidden in the back of a Mexican cart rolling for the border.'

They shook hands again. Vic said, 'You do a good job. There're some lawmen who wouldn't have given a damn what happened to an old Mexican woman. You took care of Canary, too, didn't you—with the hacksaw through the jail window?'

'Yes. I couldn't let the Hebrons butcher him. I had to do it fast and send him to you, figuring it was your job to take him from there. Where'd you bury him?'

'Amanda's bedroom closet.'

Tabor whistled softly. 'No wonder you roped trouble when Tully walked in.'

'Canary settled that with a gun after Tully knifed me.'

Tabor removed the handcuffs from the open-mouthed Canary, returned him to the room, and went to the door. 'Well, the Hebron breakup is already damned well started, Scott. Good luck. I'll do what I can.'

Vic reminded, 'I want to see Ann Lindsay.'

The morning passed and Vic slept. Later, Canary brought food and coffee from the leanto kitchen. He spoke his awed questions but Vic said, 'I'll explain later. You be ready to

217

take over a wagon and team tonight. We're getting out of the county.'

'Can't be too soon for me, Mr. Scott.'

*   *   *

His anxiety feverishly mounted as the afternoon mired to a standstill. Few sounds came inside the darkened house. Vic fitfully dozed. When his watch showed four o'clock he pulled on his boots and strapped on his shoulder gun, then his sixgun belt. Each movement was gingerly made, but the stab wound had dulled to faint throbs. Canary, white-eyed and apprehensive, had given up talking. He stirred up the cookstove coals again and brought a tin cup of coffee. Vic worried about the chimney smoke, the creepy silence, the probabilities against Tabor's being able to relay information to either Ann Lindsay or Captain Kincaid. He felt trapped. His isolation increased his doubts, his sense of futility for the showdown operation. He speculated that Ann already might be in Felix's custody and they would cross-question her about Vic Scott until her story fell to pieces.

The first small break in the waning hours of afternoon occurred when Canary agitatedly tiptoed from the kitchen and crooked a skinny finger. 'Someone at the back window!'

Drawing his gun, Vic approached the window and moved the edge of the shade. A stooped Mexican leaned against the mud wall, facing the weed-grown rear yard. The man kept his position and spoke barely loud enough for his words to come through.

'I am to say, *she is being watched, there is trouble for her to get away, you are to wait for a wagon.*'

A dozen questions tumbled through Vic's mind, wanting to be asked. But the Mexican sauntered across the yard and out of vision.

Dusk came, and at last the graveyard atmosphere was broken. Vic, on watch at the back window, saw a covered wagon roll into view. The mustang team moved at a walk. Two saddle horses trailed from lead ropes. The stooped figure of the driver sat alone on the high seat. The rig had the looks of a typical nester's outfit, with a water keg lashed to the side and the dingy swayback canvas flapping at its torn edges. When the wagon was opposite the Izaguirre house it came to a stop in the mesquites. The driver got down and began working with the lashings at the water keg. Barely discernible in the gloom, the man dropped his hand, made a waving motion, then walked to the other side of the wagon.

Vic opened the rear door. The back yards of the Mexican houses looked deserted. Canary pressed behind him.

'Walk on my left, Canary. No faster than I do. If anything starts, get down low and give me gun space.'

The walk through the weeds was the longest he had ever made. A hundred eyes seemed to bore into his back. They reached the wagon, circled behind the led horses to the off side, and the tall driver motioned with guns held in both hands.

'Right behind me,' Kincaid grunted, and climbed to the seat. Following him, Canary hastily wiggled through the wagon-cover opening. Vic followed, hardly aware of the pain produced by the exertion. In a moment he, too, sat in the tunnel of darkness in the wagon bed.

Kincaid clucked the team into motion. Over his shoulder he said, 'Take a rifle and watch the rear.'

Vic's sight adjusted to the darkness. He first saw her sitting immobile amid the jumble of bedrolls, saddles and bundled supplies. His relief was so great that his hand trembled when he picked a carbine from the floor. He crawled past her, pausing only to reach toward her hand. She grasped his own and whispered, 'Vic!—Vic!—'

He watched at the rear opening with the rifle ready. The Mexican houses receded. Then the distant lights of town vanished when the wagon dropped downgrade. Kincaid put the whip to the mustangs.

* * *

The wagon was hidden in a brush-screened

opening off the weedy wheel trace. Canary identified the location as Skull Creek, a dry ravine five miles northeast of the town and a mile south of the stage road. Beneath a shallow opening in the sandstone wall, faint light came from the coals of a small fire where Canary had cooked a scanty meal and boiled coffee. Kincaid came back from a scout of the brush south, and Vic returned from a lookout post on the ledge toward the stage road.

For the first time, Vic heard the details of their suspenseful departure from Angelo. He sat beside Ann where the fire shadows played on her face, and on the red brocaded evening bag incongruously resting in her lap.

Kincaid sat on his boot heels and blew on his coffee cup. He spoke in attempted joviality, 'Seems a shame, Scott, we got to go right back after all the trouble of getting out.'

'What time?'

'About midnight. Paul and Co. is to maneuver a raid on the railroad construction camp about then.'

Ann Lindsay said, 'I've been wanting to tell you, Captain Kincaid, that you did well, the way you got us out of town.'

Kincaid did not conceal his expression of pleasure. He told Vic, 'She knows. We exchanged a few confidences after it all came to a head.' He added gruffly, 'She made herself known to me, too. Maybe you already found out.'

She watched Vic intently. He nodded, and she said, 'You were searching my room, weren't you, when Tully came?'

'I'd just made an interesting discovery. You've been a fine actress.'

She touched the bag in her lap. 'It's in here, what you found. I had to go back for it—'

'They were watching you?'

'Yes. A Hebron man stayed on the walk in front of the hotel all afternoon. When I left for home, I knew he was following me. Captain Kincaid says we don't know whether they suspected me, or just watched to see if you tried to make contact. But it was trouble, either way. By then I had the message, a note a boy said someone paid him to deliver to me.'

'Cost me a quarter,' Kincaid said genially. 'Tabor's suggestion when he walked under my window and did some fast talking.'

'I couldn't even pack my suitcase,' Ann went on. 'Just a few things in a paper bundle. And what you saw—the leather case—' She touched the bag. 'It's in here.'

'And the little gun?' Vic smiled thinly.

'Yes. And the little gun.' She moved uneasily and watched the dying coals. 'I asked Amanda to walk back with me to the hotel, pretending I had to go back to work. She did and I think that helped put down suspicion, although the man followed us. At the door of the hotel we said good-by. She asked no questions. I think she felt that we wouldn't see each other again. The

222

Hebron man was expected to think I'd gone to work in the office for the evening. He took his stand on the porch. I slipped to the back and watched. Captain Kincaid drove through the alley, and in another minute I was in the back of the wagon and we were on our way toward the Mexican settlement.'

'It was touch and go,' Kincaid remarked. 'A woman can be a heap of trouble.' To temper that, he added judiciously, 'But this one has her wits about her.'

He stood and motioned to Canary. Each took a rifle and vanished for lookout posts in the brush.

Vic studied Ann's dark profile which showed lines of strain. She met his glance, candid and unafraid. 'I'm sure he thinks all women are weaklings and I'm an especial fool. Is that what you think, too?'

'I was thinking how much steel beneath that outward softness. Why did you do it?'

'I don't know that it was steel so much. There wasn't an hour I wasn't afraid. But I had to come here, after so much time had gone by and nobody was doing anything. When he— after I knew about it—my world came to an end. Then I got angry. Everyone had given up, I thought—his own department, the state of Texas, the law. Nobody cared, or so it seemed to me. They could let a thing like that happen and not raise a finger because the outlaws were too strong, too far away.' She added simply, 'So

223

I came.'

'That took courage.'

'I was raised on the frontier, Vic. I guess it's in my blood to fight back when there's nobody to do it for me. I had nothing better to do. I thought, if I can get in with them I will hear a careless word dropped, someone will say a name. I would have my little gun. What the federal law and Texas law had ignored, I would somehow settle. I thought they had given up, that the Hebrons were too far outside the law.'

'It was almost like that,' he conceded. 'Prez's escape set off the decision to take them on. But the federals were working on it more than you knew.'

'I've just learned that.' She searched his features for understanding. 'It makes me feel better that Drew wasn't entirely forgotten. But they would never tell *me* anything. I felt that he was wronged, that nobody cared to hunt his killers.'

'So you began with Son Hebron. And from then on they accepted you.'

'Yes. I began with Son, and Felix and Ed accepted me. Maybe I added a note of—well, respectability, you might say, to the family. Maybe they thought Son was stepping up a notch. All the time I hoped and listened and worked for any little information.'

'Did Son ever talk?'

'No specific name. I soon knew that I would never find the answer. I thought that if I could

224

get to Felix's house, search for just any clue that might suggest Drew had—had met his trouble there—'

'That explains your searching the rooms the night after Son's funeral. I thought you were really one of the family. Did you know who I was, when I first came to town?'

'I wasn't sure. I remembered your name. Drew had mentioned it to me and I knew you had been a Ranger, and his friend. I know I was secretly excited when the cattle company wrote for the hotel room for you, and on the day when you arrived. But I was not sure. You could have once been a Ranger, I thought, and had now turned into a crooked cattle buyer, ready to do business with the Hebrons. I was hoping one way, but afraid it was the other. But when they had you at Felix's, and questioned me about your past, somehow I knew, and I did my best to say something that would help.'

'You probably saved my life.'

She said earnestly, 'Vic, tell me—do you know yet? About Drew—who it was—?'

'First, you should know the U.S. Marshal's office and the state Adjutant General's department never forgot the case for one minute. You did a brave thing, foolhardy and dangerous I guess, but I can understand that. As to who it was—it was all of them, Ann. Felix, of course, is the main one, and I think Judge Ed is actually the brains for the bunch and the main reason why the law has never touched 'em. We have Canary Lenny now, who was a witness, and the federals will be able to make an indictment stand up and get a conviction. Some of them already are dead—Son, Alto and Tully. Before the night is over, we expect to have another—Prez Duvall. And maybe Judge Ed, too.'

Her hand lifted to her throat. 'For the first time, I'm ready to give up. I'm afraid of what you plan to do tonight. I just want out of the country. It's been such a long and lonely six months.'

'I've wondered,' he cautiously began, 'if there might have been one other small doubt that brought you here. A person you were curious about, as Drew's wife—'

She responded by saying honestly, 'Yes, I did wonder about Amanda Forester. The rumor came to me. I knew in my heart that it surely was something only connected with his job, what he had to do. But there is a curiosity in a woman. Call it pride, maybe. A kind of vindictive necessity to see the other woman, to know who she is and what she looks like. I guess I wanted to know the truth about that.' She added firmly, 'There may have been something intended, from Amanda's side. But for him, I know it was only a part of an undercover agent's work.'

'Of course. His job was to get in with the Hebrons, in any manner. Same as you set for yourself to do. Same as I did.'

226

She thought a moment, and said hesitantly, 'I have a message for you. When Amanda left me at the hotel she knew something was up, but not exactly what, and perhaps that we would not see each other again. She has been through so much, and still faces all the years to come out here. She just said, Vic, that if I saw you, to say, "You are an odd boarder—you never did come to my table." So I have delivered the message.'

'Maybe I should return some day,' he said dryly, 'and make amends.'

'Once she said,"We find our men and then we lose 'em." She's wise, Vic. She may secretly have guessed who I was, who Drew was—even who you are.'

Captain Kincaid emerged silently from the brush. His boot gave way on sliding gravel and he tottered before steadying himself.

'Time we start brandin', mister. You tied together enough to hang on to a horse?'

Vic moved past Ann, touching her shoulder as he did so, a gesture meant for reassurance, or good-by. Now that the time had come, he saw that her apprehension had increased. Canary brought the two horses and Kincaid instructed him to throw the saddles and bridles out of the wagon. Vic examined his guns as Canary finished the saddling job. Kincaid went over his instructions again, and concluded to Canary, 'If we're not back before false dawn, you and Ann get in this wagon and travel fast

227

out of the country. Keep in cover but go like hell and make your way to Sweetwater. From there, I reckon Mrs. Cooper knows who to notify.'

CHAPTER EIGHTEEN

Vic waited in brush concealment, checking over in his mind each small step of the details they had worked out between them on the ride in. Judge Ed's house made a low square of darkness with its inscrutable black-hooded faces for windows. The windmill made occasional fitful talk of protest.

The first problem had been the need for two more horses and Kincaid had said they simply would give Judge Ed the honor of furnishing the mounts. Vic had slipped into the barn stalls and put lead ropes on two horses. He had led these to the brush where his and Kincaid's mounts were tied. From the barn, Kincaid had lugged two sets of saddle gear and finished the job of saddling the Hebron animals.

After another whispered conference, Kincaid had ridden for town. Now Vic again tested the draw of his shoulder gun and of the .45 in his holster. He touched his weighted pockets, containing one of the two pairs of handcuffs Kincaid had brought, the folded bandanas and the rope lengths Kincaid had divided between them.

The night cooled. The usual clouds blackly piled up in the west, but a handful of stars glided in and out overhead. There was nothing to do now but watch the dark house and wait.

His worry drifted to Kincaid and what control he might hold on himself while he was in the Cactus Queen. When he pulled his mind off that, it switched to Ann Lindsay and the foolhardy but courageous compulsion that had sent her to Angelo. In contrast, he visualized Ellen Johnston in Austin, product of wealth and comforts. Out of that contrast the fact etched clear. His marriage into Judge Johnston's prestige and law practice was something that had been torn to bits and discarded forever, like Ellen's letter. Indeed, the decision had been forming itself, he admitted, from the first hours of his stagecoach journey westward to an outlaw world far distant from Austin security. The yoke he had been about to accept had been left in the greasewood barrens somewhere on the way. From the perspective of this hour of waiting, he thought wryly that Ellen, in the same hour, likely was the belle of the recurrent Austin socials, concentrating on her gown and jewels and the admiration of city eyes. That was far across the world from another woman, now hidden on brushy Skull Creek in a covered wagon, with Canary Lenny, the prairie waif, on fearful look-out, the little gun in her bag, a night of suspenseful waiting ahead.

Small sounds behind him caused his gun to whip up in his hand. Kincaid came forward. They crouched together, so near that Vic smelled the whisky.

'How did it go?'

'Good as it ever will be. Moon and Tabor came to the saloon to pick up some help. They were going to raid the railroad camp on reports that Canary was hidin' out there. That'll get the bunch away for a while. Tabor's done about all he can do.'

'Judge Ed there?'

'No sign of him. Heard that Felix's been in town. What's goin' on here?'

'No sign of life.'

'Makes it interestin', don't it? We don't know whether we got a snipe hunt yonder or a whole covey. Well, we ain't got time to find out. Let's hit 'er.'

Kincaid inched away. Vic, standing, saw Kincaid looking over the four saddle horses. Kincaid started, then changed his mind and turned back. He worked at his saddlebag. The cork made a moist snap. Kincaid raised his elbow for a long time, then lowered it, and worked the bottle back into the bag.

'Let's go, Scott.'

An angry flutter of apprehension seized Vic. He gritted, 'Goddam it, Captain—are you *sober*?'

Kincaid bristled. 'Hell, yes! This stuff don't bother me—you just worry about your own end

230

of this—'

So they started their advance in a hot rift of distrust. Warnings shrilled at Vic that they were off on the wrong foot—they should have scouted the house up close, should have circled to the far side to check for signs of horses indicating visitors. But time had pressured them for quick work. Kincaid was in no shape for this. Vic felt trapped, but Kincaid was on the move and he had to stretch his strides to keep up. He tried to detect whether Kincaid showed unbalance. But in the darkness, the tall figure beside him appeared in steady control, except for a heightened breathing.

At the bottom step of the porch, Kincaid touched his shoulder. Vic nodded and tiptoed up the steps. A porch board squeaked. Then he was pressed against the dark wall to the right of the door.

It was Kincaid's turn. He made it up the steps with no more sound than a shadow. But when he reached the door, and the next move was due, he seemed to sway slightly. He pressed his hand against the wall beside Vic and momentarily stood still. His breath sounded in shortened gasps.

Vic whispered, 'Are you all right?'

Kincaid murmured, 'Just give me a second. Felt a little dizzy.'

Desperately, Vic clutched at Kincaid's shoulder, as if to shake him. Kincaid straightened and threw off his hand. 'You get on with it—'

Vic felt for the handle of the screen door. It gave with his pull, and it opened with only the slightest squeak. He reached for the doorknob. He turned it slowly and pushed but the door failed to give. It was locked, as they had expected. So they would have to try head-on and trust to luck.

'Your move, Captain.'

Kincaid steadied himself and they exchanged places. Vic flattened to the wall beside the door.

Kincaid made his boots noisy on the floor, rattled the screen door, then pounded heavily on the facing.

'Judge Ed!' he bellowed. 'Hey! You home, Ed? You got a visitor—'

Instantaneous sounds came from inside. Footsteps moved toward the front.

A voice called, 'Who is it?' and they recognized the rasp as Ed's.

'It's me, Kincaid.'

'Who?'

'Kincaid, dammit! Got a bottle an' a deck of cards, Ed—come to see my old crony—'

They heard Judge Ed's mumble of irritation. On the other side of the door Ed called, 'Can't see you tonight, Kincaid. You go along, now.'

Kincaid laughed good-naturedly and roughly shook the doorknob. 'Aw, hell, Ed—let's liven up a dull evenin' with a little spree—'

'Can't make it, Kincaid.'

'Then, dammit, I'll rattle your doorknob till you can!'

'Get to hell gone, you drunk old bastard!' Judge Ed shouted. 'I got no time for you—'

Kincaid laughed loudly and rattled the door. Vic thought, *He's doing his act all right—but what if Ed never opens the door?*

Kincaid began a fast, rambling talk. The wait seemed an eternity. Judge Ed's protests mounted. Then Kincaid made his try with their crucial last card.

'Hey, Ed, they's big things out at the railroad camp—Canary Lenny and that other feller—'

There came a short silence. Then, as if curiosity had overwhelmed reluctance, Judge Ed turned the key and opened the door. From his position, Vic could see only the tip end of a shotgun.

Kincaid began talking again and Ed pushed the screen door ajar with the shotgun muzzle. Vic tightened his fingers on the Colt and held it shoulder high. Kincaid stepped back and Ed came another step, punching the screen with the shotgun.

'What is it they've found, Kincaid—?' He darted a glance to his left as he prodded Kincaid back. The shadow moved there. Vic swung down with the gun and steel smashed bone above Ed's ear. In unison, Kincaid stretched in a long reach and caught the shotgun before it fell, and Vic caught Ed's collapsing weight with underarm locks. He

233

pulled Ed to the side of the door and lowered him to the floor. In seconds, he snapped handcuffs on Ed's wrists pulled behind his back, pressed a folded bandana over Ed's mouth and tied it with quick twists of a length of rope.

Kincaid walked inside with both Colts raised and Vic followed.

Lamplight from an open room somewhere beyond partially outlined the front. A voice called, 'Who's out there, Ed?'

Kincaid mumbled irritably, a close enough duplication of Ed's gravel tone, 'Just that old drunk bastard—'

They started down the hallway abreast. Vic saw the open door, the yellow illumination from beyond it. *Prez, your time has come.* Just a few more steps, now. *Prez, they want you at Huntsville gallows.*

Captain Kincaid slipped on his right boot heel. As he did, he grabbed to catch himself at a small hall table. Then the table shook and gave way under his pressure. It skidded and began to fall, and Kincaid leaned with it. Too late, Vic clutched at him. Kincaid and the table crumpled together to the floor in a screech of splitting wood.

Vic heard boots thud across a floor. A form emerged to the lighted doorway. Vic saw a nightmarish image, the snarl, the scarred mouth corner, the narrowed reddish eyes, the big black gun raised in Felix's hand.

234

The three guns exploded together.

Kincaid, sprawled on the floor, had been first in Felix's line of vision and his target. Kincaid grunted and pressed his right hand to his shoulder with the smoking Colt still in it. Felix took one step and fell. Vic hurdled Kincaid's form, with his own gun still up and trailing smoke. He bounded into the room and had his first sight of Prez Duvall.

Prez was a pale, unshaven ghost, half sitting in the bed, propped on his elbow, eyes starkly white. His leg stretched outside the blanket, bandaged from ankle to thigh. In a delayed panic, Prez twisted and burrowed a hand under his pillow. Vic smashed the Colt muzzle hard into Prez's stretched neck. Prez went still, with only his mouth soundlessly working.

Roughly, Vic bent Prez's arm with a snap movement which twisted Prez to his stomach with a moan of pain. The other handcuffs were in Kincaid's pocket and he could not go for them, so Vic tore a length of rope from his pocket and bound Prez's wrists behind him. He saw that Felix had not moved. He turned back to Prez, then whirled again at sounds behind him. Kincaid tottered in the doorway, clutching at a wet stain in his shoulder.

Kincaid braced himself against the facing. Vic demanded, 'Can you make it?'

Kincaid motioned. 'No time to talk—get 'im out.'

Vic dragged Prez from the bed. 'Stand up,

Prez. Walk to the front.'

'I can't walk—'

Vic jabbed the gun into Prez's spine. Prez hobbled to the door, protesting. He looked down, snarled, 'You goddam sonsabitches!' and gingerly stepped over Felix. Kincaid stooped, braced a hand to the floor, and peered at Felix. 'He's a dead 'un. I got 'im.'

They had not counted on gunshots. Vic could only hope that they had not been heard from outside the isolated house. 'Come on, Captain—hurry!'

They paraded to the front—Prez in his union suit, dragging his leg, Vic with his gun jabbing Prez in the spine, Kincaid stumbling after.

Judge Ed was trying to raise himself from the porch floor.

'Keep a gun on Prez,' Vic said to Kincaid. He got to one knee and struggled for a lifting crotch hold on Ed, and worked him over his shoulder. His ribs seemed to tear as he lifted and straightened. After that came the nightmare of the walk across the dark yard.

With no words between them, he and Kincaid worked fast when they reached the horses. They hurried a bandana gag into Prez's mouth, tied it, and Vic added the handcuffs to Prez's wrist rope. As Prez made moaning protests, they worked him up to the saddle. Vic took another length of rope and tied his ankles tight beneath the horse's belly.

Kincaid panted. 'He nicked me, Felix did.

Losin' a little blood. But by God I took care of Felix, didn't I—?'

'Hurry, Captain. A hand now with Ed—'

But Kincaid had to lean against his horse. Again, he pressed his gun-laden fist to his shoulder. Vic single-handedly fought the weight of Judge Ed up into the saddle. Ed weakly struggled.

'It's your lookout to hang on, Judge, if you don't want to get dragged.'

He walked over to Kincaid, unable to make out his features in the dark, and Kincaid pushed back his gesture to help. Kincaid pulled himself into his saddle. The small procession was off with Vic and Kincaid each leading a horse. The night stayed quiet. The distant town lights blinked briefly through the mesquites. Vic was glad when they were lost in the distance and only a peaceful handful of stars remained.

CHAPTER NINETEEN

The wagon creaked eastward through the remaining hours of night, with Canary Lenny leading the way and riding taller in these moments of his new and important worth.

Prez Duvall and Judge Ed breathed the wagon's dust through their bandana masks, trailing on horses roped to the tailgate. Vic Scott rode behind them with a rifle across his

237

saddle, keeping an eye on the prisoners and alert to the back trail. Ann Lindsay drove the team as Canary set the course through winding cuts and stretches of brushy flats. Bedded in the wagon was Captain Kincaid. At the start, Vic had delayed only long enough to pad and bandage Kincaid's wound against blood flow, and to allow Prez to dress himself with clothes from the wagon stores.

The day hideout was made in a brush-choked ravine. Vic rode a wide circle of the camp and found no sign of pursuit. He posted Canary on a ledge to stand first watch. Taking one of his ailing prisoners at a time, he secured them with handcuffs and ropes to mesquite trunks and made a concession to their comfort by bedding them on blankets. Morose and suffering, they made no resistance. Once, Judge Ed had mumbled, dazedly, 'Felix is dead, ain't he?'

'He's dead, Judge. Felix and Tully—'

'Nobody left, hardly.' Ed closed his eyes. 'Don't know how all this happened.'

In the wagon bed, Vic rolled a side curtain to gain light. He examined Kincaid's wound again. Ann watched with concern. 'He hasn't roused all night. I'm afraid it's very bad, Vic.'

At that moment, Kincaid opened his eyes. He looked from one face to the other. He made a feeble hand gesture and his mouth wrinkled. 'I got him, didn't I, Vic?'

Vic had to bend low to catch the mumbled

238

words.

'It was my gun that got Felix Hebron, wasn't it, boy?'

If he knew that his own and Vic's gun had fired together, he was certain that only his own bullet could have felled Felix Hebron, and that was important. He waited. One eye squinted significantly at Vic, and years later Vic was to wonder if he rightly understood the old man's wink.

Vic said, 'You got him, Captain. I guess all Texas will know you did it.'

Kincaid's blood-drained features made a relaxed change. 'Been a polecat's life. Mighty lonesome.' His eyelids fluttered. 'Reckon I'll finally make the headlines on this one. You tell the Adjutant General, Vic—we busted up that bunch out yonder. Wasn't much, for old hands like us.'

He sighed, then suddenly went rigid. His chest stilled and there was no more labored breathing.

Ann covered her face with her hands and Vic gently spread a blanket over Kincaid's body.

*   *   *

In the Angelo telegraph office, Deputy Tabor composed a telegram and handed it to the operator. It read:

Stone & Chesman, Fort Worth, Texas. Your

buyer requests Angus Gilbert send riders to Sweetwater to meet him three days hence to take important delivery of livestock as planned.

He sent it unsigned, and returned to the jail office. With the death of Felix, his mission in Angelo was about concluded. He still wanted Moon, and another Hebron rider or two, if he could scheme a way to get them out of Angelo and into the custody of federal law. With discovery of what had happened at Judge Ed's house, he had planted the idea with Moon that perhaps they should get out while they had a whole skin. He could only wait to see how the suggestion had hatched. He was gratified to find Moon at his desk and see that the idea was hatching.

Moon, at mid-morning, still looked dazed. He was a man belaboring his brain toward a decision. He pushed a tortured gaze up to his deputy.

'Tabor, I been thinking. More I think, more I know it's time to get out of town for a while. No tellin' how many they got here, or when they're gonna jump me. We'd be smart to put some distance between us and Angelo.'

Tabor showed thoughtful agreement. 'I think you're right, Arch. Things don't seem healthy here, do they?'

Moon stood with decision formed. 'Let's don't fool around. Blackie and Chock want to

240

go. Don't matter about the rest out there. Everything's blowed up in their face and they'll scatter all directions. So let's the four of us ride, and damn quick.'

'Which way, Arch?'

Moon had been thinking of that, too. 'Not east, for damn sure, and not for Mexico. They don't like us down there. Opposite direction, say Amarillo first, maybe from there to Denver.'

'Amarillo would suit me,' Tabor said. 'I got some friends up that way. I could arrange for us to get in with them. Maybe some good deals.'

Moon asked hopefully, 'Would they include me in on something good, Sam? Just so it's far off and pretty safe?'

Tabor assured him with emphasis that they would. 'It would be a far piece, Arch, and you and Blackie and Chock would be absolutely safe.'

They rode from Angelo in mid-afternoon: Tabor, Moon, Blackie and Chock, well mounted and leading pack horses. As Blackie said, in four or five days of hard riding they could be safe away from the spooky business in Angelo. And damn lucky to get away, without going the bloody route of Felix and Tully and Alto. None suggested that they search for Judge Ed and Prez. Whatever happened to them was their own hard luck—this was a case of every man for himself.

241

*   *   *

The Texas Ranger contingent responding to Tabor's message took over the prisoners in Sweetwater, placed Prez and Ed in jail under twenty-four-hour guard, and arranged for the funeral service for Captain Kincaid. The service had been simple graveside rites with six of his fellow Rangers and a few townspeople in attendance. Afterward, Vic, Canary and Ann slept a day through.

A doctor treated Vic's wound. The weekly newspaper editor sent the news pouring eastward by telegraph. Two telegrams came for Vic. The one from the Adjutant General he carefully folded and placed in his wallet with a surge of pride. The one from Ellen Johnston he thoughtfully tore to bits and, without emotion, let scatter out the window on the wings of a red, swirling sandstorm.

The following day, Vic and Ann Lindsay sat in the hotel lobby talking with Ranger Captain Bert Frazer.

Frazer asked idly, 'What's next for you, Scott? I've heard you might be thinking of quitting the force and goin' into law practice in Austin.'

Vic glanced at Ann who evaded his eyes.

'I don't know, Bert,' he said uncomfortably. 'Things have changed a little since I started on this case.'

Jovially, Bert said, 'Sure have. You're goin'

to be right famous in the Special Service detail, ain't he, Mrs. Cooper? When he gets back to headquarters they'll likely give him a promotion and any assignment he wants.'

Undercover is a lonely life, Kincaid had said.

Bert Frazer stood, significantly looked at Vic, and made a motion toward the entrance to the hotel bar. Vic rose and started to follow him. He glanced down and saw Ann's direct glance studying him.

Vic said, 'You should be well acquainted in Fort Worth. In case I decided to make a change, maybe you could introduce me to someone to help me get a job. One where I could still study law on the side.'

'Why, yes, Vic.' Her eyes held unwaveringly on him. 'You might make a connection with the place where I worked, before I decided to go to Angelo.'

'And where was that?'

Her mouth barely narrowed, making a faint dimple wrinkle at the corner. 'I was an office clerk.' She paused. 'I think my firm would be interested in having you join them—'

'A legal firm?'

'No, Vic. I was a clerk in the office of Stone and Chesman.'

He stared at her.

She said, 'I hope I can get my old place back with them. And I imagine they can always use an honest commission buyer.'

He stalked to the bar entrance and joined

Captain Frazer. They ordered whisky and Frazer asked curiously, 'How'd you first stumble on to Drew Cooper's widow out at Angelo?'

Vic tried to think back, across the time that had been so brief, yet so eternally long. 'Why, I met her at a place,' he said slowly, lifting his glass. 'It's known out there as Hooligan's Corral.'

He paused with the drink, murmured, 'To Captain Kincaid,' and Bert softly said, 'Amen,' and then they stood a moment, savoring the biting warmth going down.

'Fill 'em again?' asked the barkeep.

A rasping old voice spoke affirmatively from somewhere. The barkeep was looking curiously at Vic, and Vic looked at Frazer; but Frazer was waiting, and Vic said hoarsely, 'Did you say something, Bert?' Bert shook his head and muttered, 'I thought you did.' The barkeep must have heard it, too, for he poured the shot glasses to the brim.